UP WEST

CHAPTER C

It was the summer of 1989 in Drapov, the c[a]... European country. Frank and Theodor, two f... afternoon. A bird flew overhead as bright sun shine illuminated the two thirsty men. The street was bustling with people as they were engaged in their daily affairs. Frank and Theodor, who had both reached their thirties, watched the world pass by.

"Waitress!" called Theodor, who regarded her with his blue eyes. He had fair hair and was dressed in a sandy coloured suit.

"Can I help you?" asked the waitress, a brown eyed brunette, stopping at their table.

"Certainly. Two ales, please."

"Coming right up, handsome!" She made a note and entered the cafe.

"Do you know much about the Secret Police?" asked Frank, who had hazel eyes, black hair and wore a beige suit.

"A little. Why do you want to know?" inquired Theodor, raising his eyebrows.

"I'm just curious."

Austin, a short man wearing spectacles who was seated at a nearby table, listened to the conversation. He had had brown eyes, was slightly bald and wore a brown suit. He was in his forties and pretended to read a newspaper.

"You have a good life, Frank. You are a successful history lecturer and have a wife to look after you. Don't pry into matters that could land you in trouble," said Theodor.

"You're being evasive," said Frank.

"True, but I want to protect you. I don't want the Secret Police to arrest you at 3 o'clock in the morning and steal you into the night."

"I'm sure that wouldn't occur."

"You'd be surprised!"

The waitress arrived with the two ales on a tray and placed them on the table.

"That was quick!" said Theodor.

"I'm a fast worker," she replied, smiling.

"Here you are and keep the change."

"Thank you."

The waitress walked over to Austin.

"Tonic water, please," he said, cheered up by her presence.

"Fine," she nodded and returned to the cafe.

"So, how is life treating you?" asked Frank, stretching his arms.

"Things could be better. A lot better," replied Theodor, rolling his eyes upwards.

"You are disillusioned."

"Sure. I might leave Malvaria and live in Western Europe."

"You think you might be happier there?"

"Yes. I'd have more freedom. I'm sick of communism because it just means bureaucracy. All this red tape is strangling me."

"You don't want to pursue the common good?"

"The common good? Nobody believes in these noble political ideals. They just pay lip service to it. It's all a facade."

"Do you think democracy is superior to communism?"

"Despite its imperfections, democracy is more fun than communism. At least you get decent night clubs in the West."

"Is that all that matters to you? Having fun?"

"I would enjoy greater quality of life in the West – plus a higher salary. I'm tired of living here."

The two men continued conversing until they finished their drinks. They bid farewell and departed, as the sun hid behind a cloud. Frank looked at his watch and decided to head home. He walked down a cobbled street and noticed Austin was following him. The lecturer turned a corner, then confronted the other man.

"You were following me," said Frank, towering over the man.

"You were waiting for me," replied Austin.

"What do you want?"

"You're a historian. An academic."

"How do you know?"

"You're friend said so – in the cafe."

"Don't waste my time," said Frank, walking off.

"You mentioned an interest in the Secret Police."

Frank stopped and turned around.

"You know about them?"

"I am a Detective in the Secret Service, our proper name."

"Prove it."

"You are a cautious man. Here is my identification."

Austin passed Frank his badge, which he examined and returned.

"Detective Austin Malkopf. What business do you have with me?" asked Frank who was suspicious of the powerful man before him.

"I have something you want – and you have something I want."

"Such as?"

"I have information about the Secret Service – and you, Frank, are an eminent man, a historian."

"You want to make use of me?"

"You are an intelligent man and I suspect you support the Communist Party."

"That is correct."

"In that case, if you help the Secret Police, you assist the communists."

"How can I help you?"

"The winds of change are blowing in our direction. The people of Malvaria hear stories about Western Europe – and they want to wear denim jeans. The government is becoming increasingly unpopular, therefore the Communist Party could benefit with someone like you on their side."

"And if I do not co-operate?"

"You may return to your life. Now, I must go. If you wish to discuss this matter further, meet me at the fountain in Capital Park. Is tomorrow at 8pm a suitable time?

"Yes."

"Goodbye, then"

The two men departed. Frank continued his journey home and soon reached the block of flats where he lived. He entered the building via the main doors, then ascended the stairs. Two boys passed him, chattering and laughing. He walked over to his front door and entered the flat. He hung up his coat in the hall, then entered the kitchen.

"Hi Alexis," he said to his wife. She had blue eyes and long, brunette hair. She wore a blouse, a short skirt and sensible shoes. Plus she was in her thirties.

"Where have you been?" she asked, looking rather vexed.

"Do I get a kiss?"

"Tell me where you've been first."

"I was having a drink with Theodor."

"I thought as much."

"We only had one."

"You don't deserve a kiss!"

"I'm sorry I 'm late, Alexis."

"Don't make a habit of it."

"Is my supper ready?"

"It's in the oven."

. Frank opens the oven door, removes a dish and places it on a kitchen surface.

"Beef stroganoff, my favourite!"

"I've already eaten. I dislike waiting for people."

Frank ate his meal, watched television with Alexis, then they retired to bed.

CHAPTER TWO

In the morning, Frank rose from his bed and freshened up in the bathroom. He shared breakfast with Alexis, then walked to the University where he spent the day teaching. After supper with Alexis, Frank left the flat and met Marius, a neighbour, on the landing. Marius's brown eyes were visible behind his spectacles. He had grey hair and wore a cardigan, a patterned shirt, casual trousers and well worn shoes. He had recently reached fifty.

"Good evening, Frank," said Marius, smiling.

"Good evening, Marius," said Frank, wearily.

"How are you and the lovely Alexis?"

"We're fine. We had a dispute last night, but we patched things up today."

"I am glad to hear that. Alexis is a fire cracker!"

"She speaks her mind."

"Don't worry. As she grows older, she will lose her passion."

"How is Matilda?"

"My wife is inside cooking supper. She knows what's best."

"I will see you later."

Frank descended the stairs and left the building. He walked over to Capital Park and arrived at the fountain. He glanced at his watch: it was 8 o'clock. He looked around and observed Austin was approaching him.

"Good evening," greeted Austin, smiling.

"Austin," replied Frank.

They shook hands.

"The fountain is beautiful," said Austin, then gestured towards a bench. "Let's sit over there."

The two men sat on the bench, as a boy cycled past.

"I am not sure I should be here," said Frank, feeling troubled.

"Man stands between certainty and uncertainty," said Austin. "Still, if you want to you may leave."

"No, tell me about the Secret Service."

"The aim of the Secret Service is to enable the ruling party to retain power. Our head quarters are in the city. We survey people who pose a threat to the government and our operations are covert. We repress dissidents who may weaken the political power of the Communist Party. Now then, I want you to help us."

"How?"

"It has been brought to the attention of my superiors that, at the University, a political entity called the Democratic Party has sprung up, involving academics and students."

"I wouldn't worry too much about the students. They have trouble getting up before midday."

"This is not a time for jollity. I want information: the names of party members, times and localities of meetings, their plans for the future."

"I can manage that."

"Excellent. I will give you a week to investigate the Democratic Party."

"What shall I do?"

"Think man! Be discreet. Casually ask about the Democratic Party at the University until you meet someone who knows about it. Take steps to attend one of their meetings. Use your eyes and ears. Observe and listen."

"What if they suspect me?"

"They have no reason to suspect you so just act naturally."

"I have never been a spy before."

"You will be a messenger – for the most rational ideology on earth – communism. Please type up your information for me. I will meet you here in seven days at 8 o'clock so don't be late."

Austin stands up and walks off. By chance, Theodor is in the park and notices Frank by the fountain. They greet each other.

"Frank, I didn't expect to see you here," said Theodor.

"Hi, I came out for a walk," said Frank, standing up.

"Who was that? He looked very earnest," commented Theodor, gesturing towards Austin.

"Him? He just wanted some directions – to City Hall."

Theodor wore a doubtful expression and shrugged his shoulders.

"Talking of City Hall, I must visit the place soon myself," he continued.

"Why is that?"

"I want to emigrate and I need to pick up the necessary papers."

"It is difficult to emigrate from Malvaria."

"It is difficult but not impossible. Still, if the government won't allow me to, I'll find a way to break out."

"That's dangerous."

"Where there's a will there's a way."

"What would you do in a western country?"

"Don't worry about me. I'll land on my own two feet. I always do."

The two men strolled around the Park whilst they engaged in conversation. They passed a young couple holding hands. After a while, Frank and Theodor returned to their respective homes.

CHAPTER THREE

Frank was sat at his desk in his room at the University with four male students in their early twenties. They had just finished a tutorial in which they had been discussing the history of Malvaria. They looked forward to some light refreshment.

"So I'll see you next week. Same time, same place. And don't forget your assignments."

The students put their books into their bags and three of them departed from the room.

"How's it going, Leopold?" asked Frank.

"Everything's fine," replied Leopold, who possessed green eyes, short brown hair and wore spectacles. His clothing included a t shirt, light blue jeans and trainers.

"Are we keeping you busy with academic work?"

"Certainly."

Leopold walked to the door.

"What about extra-curricular activities? Have you joined a society?" inquired Frank.

"No, not yet," replied the student. He walked over to Frank. "I have joined a political party."

"Which one?"

"A group of lecturers and students have formed the Democratic Party, although it is unauthorised by the government."

"Tell me about it."

"We're not supposed to."

"You can trust me."

"Well...all right. Our aim is to bring democracy to Malvaria and westernise it. We want a different way of life."

"How will you achieve that?"

"It sounds like you are interested in the Democratic Party."

"That is correct. Could I attend a meeting?"

"I'm not sure. We have to be secretive."

"I won't tell a soul."

"Well, we could benefit from new members."

"I won't let you down."

"We have a meeting tonight. But make sure you don't tell anyone. We don't want the government to find out about us – and send the Secret Police to arrest us."

"There's no need to worry about that. So where is the meeting?"

"We will be upstairs at the Blue Boar tonight at 8 o'clock. But remember this – the Democratic Party will be unforgiving to anyone who betrays us."

Later on that night, Frank explained to Alexis that he was going out for a drink with some work colleagues. He departed from the flat and walked to the bar. It was an old building with the sound of customers chatting and bustling inside. Frank took a deep breath, looked from left to right, then entered.

Inside the Blue Boar, the crowd was friendly and cordial. Frank looked around to see Leopold sitting at a table in a corner with some colleagues. The student noticed Frank so he walked over to him and they shook hands.

"I'm so glad you could make it," said Leopold, smiling.

"Good evening," said Frank.

"Would you like a drink?"

"Don't worry, I'll order one."

"If you insist! We'll chat here first, then move to a room upstairs in a short while. But be careful, don't discuss the Party here, we will talk about it when we go upstairs. Walls have ears."

Frank walked over to the bar with the student.

"What would you like, sir?" asked the young barmaid.

"An ale, please. Leopold?" asked Frank.

"Nothing. I already have a drink," replied the student.

Frank looked around.

"I recognize some of your colleagues," he said.

"Yes. That's Stefan, the philosophy lecturer. It's scandalous, he's never read Hegel," said Leopold.

"That accounts for his cheerful, untroubled expression. And that's Hammond."

"Of course. He teaches politics, but none of the students understand him."

"Neither do the lecturers. And there is Sabrina."

"You're right. I'm not sure what she teaches."

"Neither is she."

"She is a feminist. She represents women...or something like that."

""Here is your drink, sir," said the barmaid.

"Thank you very much," said Frank.

The two men walked over to the group in the corner.

"Attention everyone. This is Frank, my tutor," announced Leopold."He will be joining our meeting later on, unless anyone objects, of course."

"Can we trust him?" asked Sabrina, viewing him suspiciously with her piercing blue eyes. Her hair was turning grey and she wore a red dress with black shoes.

"Sabrina!" protested Hammond, rolling his green eyes upwards. His short hair was brown and was a similar colour to his casual suit. Plus he wore a pair of brogues.

"Well, he is a man, after all!" said Sabrina.

"Sure, we can trust Frank, even though he is a man. You have my word," reassured Leopold."I told him about the...Party."

"We must be careful. We live in dangerous times," said Hammond, widening his eyes.

"But there is change in the air, I can feel it," said Stefan, clenching his fist.

"Hush! We must talk about these matters upstairs, where it is safe!" said Sabrina, pointing her finger upwards.

"Hi, Frank," said a female student, waving flirtatiously. She looked at him with her brown eyes, fluttering her long black eye lashes, which matched the colour of her hair, which was in a bob. She wore denim dungarees and ankle boots.

"Hello," said Frank, rather taken aback by this attention.

"Excuse me, I should introduce you to everyone," remarked Leopold, raising his eyebrows at the young woman's behaviour."This is Melissa, a literature student. She's cute, but she's never handed an essay in on time!"

"Well, there's so much to do at University, like going out and having a good time!" said Melissa, beaming.

"Hedonists!" declared Leopold. "This is Nickolas, a philosophy student."

"I am pleased to meet you," said Nickolas, whose face featured blue eyes plus he had brown, short hair. He wore a t shirt with a giant question mark on the front, plus a pair of khaki trousers and desert boots.

"This is Hugh, he is a forward looking history student," continued Leopold.

"Hi," said Hugh, slightly bemused by Leopold's comment. Hugh wore spectacles in front of his brown eyes. He had fair, short hair, plus he wore a chequered shirt, blue trousers and black shoes.

"I think you know the lecturers, Stefan, Hammond and Sabrina," said Leopold.

"Good evening, Frank! Take a seat!" urged Sabrina, enthusiastically.

Frank and Leopold sat down.

"What do you teach?" asked Melissa with a happy expression.

"History," replied Frank.

"Wow! I've always been interested in tales of yester year, too!"

"Quite!"

"Stop flirting, Melissa!" said Sabrina, with a vexed look.

"I was not! I was only being friendly!" retorted Melissa.

"I think we should move upstairs," said Hammond.

"But Frank and Leopold have only just sat down," commented Sabrina.

"Really, I don't object to moving," said Frank.

"Time is of the essence," said Hammond, observing his watch.

"I agree. Let's go upstairs," said Leopold.

Hammond walked over to a closed door to be followed by the others. He pointed upwards to the barman, a middle aged man, who nodded. Hammond opened the door and the group entered a hallway.

"You must understand, we have to be secretive. The Communist Party does not take kindly to opposition," said Hammond.

"Don't worry, I understand," replied Frank, as the group ascended a stairway.

"Does anyone know you are here?"

"I told my wife I was going out for a drink with colleagues from the University."

"Good. It's best she does not know the whole truth for her safety and ours."

"Don't go on like that," said Sabrina.

"I will, Sabrina, I will," replied Hammond.

He reached the landing and opened a door; he entered the room to be followed by the others. Here there was a table surrounded by chairs. Hammond walked over to a window and looked outside. He saw lit streetlamps, closed shops, people travelling by foot and a van passed by.

"It's quiet outside and I think we are secure here," he said.

Everybody sat down, then Hammond dealt some playing cards.

"What are the cards for?" inquired Frank, rather puzzled.

"We're not really here to form the Democratic Party, we're here to play cards," declared Leopold, giggling.

"I beg your pardon," said Frank, confused.

"He's only joking," said Stefan, reassuringly. "If we're busted by the Secret Police, we'll say we're playing poker and hope for the best."

"We must start the meeting and begin in earnest," asserted Hammond, looking at everyone.

"Here, here," agreed Leopold, waving his fist in the air.

"The fact is the Communist Party, the government, yields too much power. They control industry, agriculture, education, the health service, the police, the army. In short, they control everything," said Hammond.

"They have abolished the freedom of speech. What we are saying now is forbidden," said Stefan, shrugging his shoulders.

"They have spies everywhere. No one is safe," added Hammond.

Frank felt uneasy, but continued to listen.

"Our artists live under state censorship and political dissidence is not tolerated," said Stefan.

"And I can't find the right shampoo and conditioner for my hair!" announced Melissa, scowling.

"Melissa!" said Leopold.

"She's right! The range of consumer goods is limited! These factors have caused social discontent," explained Hammond.

"You want to turn Malvaria into a giant shopping centre?" questioned Frank in dismay.

"It is time to westernize the country and set up a democratic government," said Leopold.

"We need to give the people human rights and the freedoms enjoyed by Western countries," said Stefan.

"We need political reform..." suggested Frank.

"Reform?" asked Sabrina.

"It would be a mistake to fully westernize the country," said Frank, feeling aggravated.

"Why, god damn it?" asked Sabrina, slamming the table.

"Because then we would inherit the ills of Western countries," argued Frank.

"Like what?" asked Sabrina.

"The country would be cursed by capitalism and become a consumer society. The people will become passive consumers, obsessed with sex, trivia and celebrity."

"I can't wait!" declared Melissa.

"If we Westernize Malvaria, the people will become materialistic," said Frank.

"You are prejudging the future," said Sabrina.

"The dependence on market forces will lead to financial and social insecurity, causing crime," said Frank.

"You are reaching narrow conclusions," suggested Hammond.

"If you want to talk about spiritual values, look at what has happened to the country: the Church has been brought under communist control in order to replace Christian values with communist values. This is an example of thought control," said Hugh.

"The question is: are you with us or against us?" asked Hammond.

"As I said, I believe in reform, but not total change," concluded Frank.

"It would be good to have Frank at our meetings. After all, our aim is not to dissolve the Communist Party, but to establish democracy including the communists," said Leopold.

"It would be good to have a voice of dissent at our meetings. We believe in the freedom of speech," said Sabrina.

A while later, the meeting drew to a close and the group discretely dispersed. Outside the Blue Boar, Frank talked to Leopold.

"Thank you for coming to the meeting. What did you think of it?" asked Leopold.

"It was intriguing. I must return home now because it's late," replied Frank.

"Will you attend the next meeting? We need as much support as we can get."

"Yes, I will see you at the next one. When is it?"

"Same time next week. But remember, keep quiet about it."

"Of course."

The lecturer and the student departed. Frank walked back to his flat and soon entered the bedroom. Alexis was sitting in bed with a vexed expression as she read a novel.

"Good evening," said Frank.

"Is it?" retorted Alexis.

"What's the matter, my love?"

"Don't worry about me. You make sure you have a good time at the bar while I read a romantic novel at home."

"I had important matters to discuss."

"Like what?"

"University matters."

"What about us?"

"I'll make it up to you."

"Don't bother."

"I'll sleep on the sofa."

Frank left the bedroom, entered the lounge and stepped onto the balcony. He viewed the street below, then looked up at the night sky as it started to rain.

"Bloody hell!" he said.

CHAPTER FOUR

The next day, Frank stood outside a popular book shop, admiring the window display. There was a poster advertising a signing by a renowned author the following Saturday. The lecturer entered the shop to begin browsing in the hope of finding an inspiring book to read. Theodor entered the shop by chance and spotted his friend, whom he approached from behind. Theodor grabbed Frank's shoulders to surprise him.

"Boo!" said Theodor and startled Frank, who turned around.

"Theodor! It would be you!" said Frank.

"Frank! What are you looking for? The Illustrated Lolita?"

"No, they don't appear to have that!"

"What a shame! So, how's it going, my friend?"

"Not bad. Well, quite bad."

"What's happened?"

"Alexis and I had a bust up last night. I slept on the sofa."

"But Alexis is a wonderful person! You must make it up to her!"

"How?"

"Buy her some flowers, you fool!"

"That sounds reasonable. How about you?"

"Me? I have filled in my emigration papers and handed them to City Hall."

"How long is the process?"

"A few months."

"Good luck."

"Still, I must return to work."

"Sure, I'll see you."

"Goodbye."

Theodor left the shop and Frank continued browsing. Later on, Frank entered a florist and purchased a bunch of flowers. He returned home where he ascended the stairs to his flat. Here he encountered Marius.

"Good evening," greeted Frank.

"Frank, you needn't have bothered," said Marius, smiling.

"The flowers are not for you."

"Of course, I'm only kidding."

"They're for Alexis. We had a bust up."

"You must look after her. After all, you don't want to lose her. Trust me, you won't find a better cook."

"You're right there."

"Still, have a good evening and please – cheer up!"

Marius descended the stairs as Frank reached the top. The lecturer entered the flat and walked into the hall.

"I'm home, my love," he said, then entered the kitchen to see Alexis cooking. He handed her the flowers. "These are for you."

Alexis's face lit up. She received the flowers and smelt them.

"Goodness! Whose idea was that?" she asked.

"It was my idea."

"You've improved!"

Alexis put the flowers into a colourful vase and placed them on the table.

"I've cooked you a stew, although I'm not sure you deserve it."

"Thank you. I thought maybe we could go out one night, like we used to."

"Sure. What about tomorrow night?"

"Not tomorrow night. I have to meet someone."

"What for?"

"University matters."

"It's always university matters."

"What about the night after tomorrow?"

"Is that a promise?"

"Yes, I promise."

"I'll hold you to that."

The couple soon enjoyed the stew and discussed their proposed night out. They went out for a walk over to Capital Square, then returned home. After a light supper, they watched TV and retired to bed.

CHAPTER FIVE

The following evening arrived on time, so Frank walked over to Capital Park. He reached the main gates and entered. It was fairly warm in the Park, although there were not many people around. Frank walked over to the fountain where he checked his watch, then noticed Austin approaching, carrying a brown leather briefcase.

"Austin," said Frank.

"Good evening. Did you manage to acquire information about the Democratic Party?" asked Austin.

"Yes. I attended a meeting a few nights ago. Here are my notes. I typed them up in my office for you."

Austin took the notes and looked through them, pleased by what he saw.

"Excellent. The quality of your information is good. I'm sure the Communist Party will be pleased," commented Austin.

"Good," said Frank.

"Would you be willing to offer your services again?"

"Yes, I'll attend another one of their meetings in a few days."

"Brilliant. In that case, I'll see you here same time next week."

Austin put the notes into his briefcase, as Frank departed. Soon, Austin walked away from the fountain, pleased with Frank's co-operation.

CHAPTER SIX

A new evening occurred and Frank was standing on the balcony to his flat. Down below a car containing young people passed by, emitting the sound of loud pop music. Frank temporarily recalled being young, then entered the lounge. Alexis appeared from the hall.

"Are you ready yet?" asked Frank, conscious of the time.

"Please be patient. I'm nearly ready," replied Alexis.

"I'm sorry. It's just that I booked us a table at the restaurant and I don't want to be late."

"It won't matter if we're a little late. How do I look?"

"You look great."

"Thank you. I hope you mean it!"

"You've never looked better."

"I'll just look in the mirror and brush my hair...Fine! Let's go now. We don't want to be too late."

The couple took a taxi to the restaurant, which was called Number 68. They entered and a waiter guided them to their table. They sat down, then ordered from the menu. The restaurant was busy plus the sound of chatter was continuous. Soon the couple began to eat their starters.

"How is yours?" asked Frank, feeling rather jovial.

"It's delicious. How is yours?" inquired Alexis, glancing at his plate.

"They've given me too many vegetables."

"Always complaining!"

"I am not!"

"You are, too! Oh dear. Here comes your alcoholic friend."

Theodor approached the table, looking flustered, unhappy and desperate. He was aware the couple would be dining there as Frank happened to mention it to him earlier in the week. Theodor wiped his brow and focussed his attention on Frank, who wondered what the difficulty was. Alexis was quite bemused.

"Frank," said Theodor.

"Good evening," replied Frank.

"Hi Alexis," said Theodor.

"Hi," she replied.

"Alexis says you are my alcoholic friend," said Frank.

"Nonsense," said Theodor.

"Come off it, you drink like a fish," claimed Alexis.

"I've never seen a fish drink beer," asserted Theodor.

"You look distressed. Tell me, what's the matter?" asked Alexis.

"I have some bad news," said Theodor.

"You only have two weeks to live?" inquired Alexis.

"No, it's not that bad. My application for emigration to Western Europe has been rejected by the authorities," said Theodor.

"What a shame!" quipped Alexis.

"Alexis!" said Frank. "Why was your application rejected?"

"I don't know because the letter didn't say. It's so typical of this country," grumbled Theodor.

"You and me will have to find out. We can visit City Hall with the letter," said Frank.

"That's good of you," said Theodor.

"When do you want to meet there?" asked Frank.

"What about tomorrow at lunchtime?" inquired Theodor.

"Say twelve o'clock?" suggested Frank.

"Good. I will see you then," said Theodor.

Theodor departed from the restaurant, hoping his life would improve. Frank and Alexis discussed their friend's dilemma, finished their meals, then settled the bill. They soon returned home to bed.

CHAPTER SEVEN

The next day appeared and Theodor walked towards the City Hall with a sense of purpose. It was sunny with a few clouds in the sky. Frank was waiting outside the building, which was impressive with a range of pillars at the entrance. Theodor met Frank, they nodded at each other meaningfully, then entered the building. Once inside, they approached the reception. The interior to the building had good air conditioning, so the two men felt cool.

"Good afternoon, can I help?" asked Ira, the receptionist. She was in her twenties and viewed the two men with her blue eyes. Her long hair was blond and she wore a long, light blue dress with black slip-on shoes.

"Yes, I received a letter from the Emigration Office informing me that I am not eligible for emigration to Western Europe," said Theodor.

"May I see the letter?"

"Yes. Here it is."

"The documentation is official."

"Of course."

"Why have you come here?"

"Because I want to know why my application has been rejected."

"I have no idea. The reason is not stated in the letter."

"Who can give me a reason?"

"The letter is signed by Hilda Page, an Emigration Officer. Can we speak with her?" asked Frank.

"Possibly," said Ira.

"Possibly?"

"There is no need to become angry, sir."

"Earlier you offered us your help," said Theodor, firmly.

"If you are going to raise your voice with me, I will have to ask you to leave the building," said Ira.

"Please, can we speak with Hilda Page?" asked Frank.

"Wait one moment," said Ira. She speaks on a nearby 'phone:"Good afternoon, may I speak with Hilda Page...I have a gentleman who would like to speak with you. His name is on the letter...Theodor Rushkin. His application for emigration has been rejected...You may speak with Mrs Page in the Emigration Office."

"Can my friend come?" asked Theodor.

"Yes. Turn up that corridor, the Office is the third door on the left," said Ira.

"Thank you," said Theodor.

The two men walked up the corridor to the Emigration Office. Here Theodor knocked at the door, but no one answered. He knocked once more and Hilda opened the door.

"Good afternoon, Mr Rushkin?" inquired Hilda with a slight smile.

"Yes, Mrs Page, and this is my friend, Frank Vockins," said Theodor.

"Come in," said Hilda, nodding.

Theodor and Frank entered the office, which was large with bookshelves as well as filing cabinets. Hilda wore a green dress with shiny shoes and was in her fifties. She wore spectacles plus she had brown eyes and hair. She looked through a filing cabinet near to her desk.

"Theodor Rushkin, Theodor Rushkin...Ah, here we are," said Hilda. She smiled, removed a file, walked over to the desk and sat down."Please be seated."

The two men complied.

"Mr Rushkin, you applied for emigration to Germany and were declined," began Hilda.

"Yes, I want to know why. You've only had the emigration papers a few days...," said Theodor.

"The government is not allowing anyone to leave at the moment, except in rare circumstances. Malvaria needs you."

"Sorry?"

"You are an insurance clerk, a valuable and much needed citizen here."

"But what about my wishes?"

"Malvaria requires your expertise. Germany has plenty of insurance clerks."

"I want to emigrate and start a new life."

"You live in a communist state and the state is more important than the individual."

"This is ridiculous."

"I disagree. This is all perfectly rational."

Theodor stands up and puts his hands on the table.

"I want you to change your mind," he said.

"No, my decision is final. Now if you don't mind, I have lots of work to do," said Hilda.

"This is my life we're talking about."

"I bid you good day."

Frank stood up.

"Come on. Let's go," he said.

The two friends left the Office and Theodor slammed the door shut.

"Tut, tut," said Hilda, raising her eyebrows.

Frank and Theodor walked down the corridor, observing the framed prints reflecting communist life on the walls. Potted plants were neatly arranged here and there. Ornate chandeliers hung from the ceiling.

"She referred to the state. Well, the state is driving me crazy," remarked Theodor, scratching his head.

"I sympathize...The communists don't want people to leave or enter," commented Frank.

"I have to get out. I have to."

"Keep your voice down. We're in City Hall."

"What am I going to do?"

"I may be able to help. I'll talk to you where it's safe."

The two men left the building, then walked down two streets. Along the way, they passed a young woman playing the violin and each threw some money into her empty case. She smiled, carrying on her performance. The two friends reached the Clock Tower and looked around.

"We can talk here. No one can hear us," said Frank.

"You said you could help me," said Theodor.

"Yes, I attended a meeting of the Democratic Party last week."

"I didn't know such a party existed."

"They have to be secretive, but they may be able to help."

"How?"

"They may be able to help you cross the border without the permission of the authorities."

"That's dangerous."

"True, but I'll hear what they have to say."

"How did you find out about them?"

"One of my students is a member and I found out through him."

"I see. But I thought you sympathized with the communists."

"That's right, I did, but it may be time for the country to move towards democracy. A lot of people are unhappy under communist rule."

"You're right there. Still, I have to go now."

"Sure, I'll catch you later."

The two men departed in a hopeful mood. Up above, the clouds slowly dispersed, exposing the sun. Nearby, the violinist ended her final performance and returned home.

CHAPTER EIGHT

It was the evening for the following meeting of the Democratic Party. Frank stood outside the Blue Boar, wondering what to expect. A young couple entered the bar as a cool breeze passed Frank. He too stepped into the old building. He approached the varnished, wooden bar and met Leopold.

"Good evening," said Leopold.

"How are you?" asked Frank.

"Not bad at all. And you?"

"I have a proposal to make which I will air upstairs."

"How intriguing."

Hammond approached them.

"Frank, we are going upstairs now," he said.

"Sure. I will order a drink. An ale, please," asked Frank.

"Of course," said the barmaid.

Hammond approached the doorway and ascended the stairs.

"What kind of proposal is it?" inquired Leopold.

"It involves a friend of mine who needs some help," explained Frank.

"There you are, sir," said the barmaid, handing Frank his drink.

"Thanks," said Frank, smiling.

Frank and Leopold walked over to the doorway, then ascended the stairs. Soon they entered the meeting room upstairs, where Hammond was looking out onto the street below. A few people strolled past and a sports car sped by.

"I can't spot anyone watching the building, so we seem to be safe," remarked Hammond, reassuring everyone.

All the members of the Democratic Party were assembled. They exchanged pleasantries, discussed problems and so on. Soon enough, everyone had sat down.

"Good evening everyone and welcome to another meeting of the Democratic Party," greeted Hammond, surveying everyone.

"Frank has a proposal to make," declared Leopold.

"Indeed. What is it?"

"A friend of mine, Theodor, wishes to emigrate to Germany, but the government won't let him," said Frank.

"How does that affect us?" asked Hammond.

"I hoped the Party could help him... to escape," said Frank.

"You mean illegally?" asked Hammond.

"Yes, if necessary," said Frank.

"What does everyone think?" asked Hammond, hoping for a discussion.

"Why won't the government let him emigrate?" asked Sabrina.

"The Emigration Officer said he is need by the state. He is an insurance clerk," divulged Frank.

"Can we help him legally?" asked Sabrina.

"There is little we can do," said Hammond, shaking his head. "The authorities are inflexible."

"It would be dangerous to assist him illegally," suggested Hugh.

"Don't be so mean spirited, you creep," asserted Melissa.

"I am only thinking of the preservation of the Party. How are we meant to defeat the communists if we all end up in jail by trying to help one person to jump the border?" asked Hugh.

"He has a point," said Stefan.

"The aim of the Party is to liberate the people of Malvaria. Therefore the interests of the people outweigh the interests of one person," said Hugh.

"I think the Party should help him and take action," said Melissa.

"It would be a very hazardous and highly risky venture," said Hugh.

"You coward," snapped Melissa.

"I am only being sensible and putting the interests of the Party and the people first. Besides, how do we enable him to leave the country?" asked Hugh.

"My boyfriend, Reuben, owns a private aeroplane. He may be able to help," said Melissa.

"That sounds like a reasonable idea," said Sabrina.

"What does everyone think?" asked Hammond.

"I believe our main aim should be to overthrow the government. Then we can ease emigration laws," said Hugh.

"How do we overthrow the government?" asked Nickolas.

"We organise a protest march in Drapov and express our views," said Hugh.

"That is a good strategy," said Hammond.

"A protest march won't guarantee results," said Melissa.

"If we arrange a protest march with thousands of students, the government will have to listen to us," said Hugh.

"What is your view?" Hammond asked Frank.

"My friend is keen to leave the country, whereas a protest march will take time to organise and may not be successful," replied Frank.

"I can bring Reuben along to the next meeting so we can discuss this issue further," Melissa.

"I will discuss this with Theodor and bring him to the next meeting as well," said Frank.

The meeting lasted a while longer, then drew to a close. Everyone departed with stimulated minds, looking forward to the next gathering of the Democratic Party. Frank met up with Leopold outside.

"What did you think of tonight's meeting?" asked the student.

"It went well," replied the lecturer.

"I hope we can help your friend."

"He's reached the end of his tether, living here in Malvaria."

"Don't worry. We will soon be a democracy, provided the Secret Police don't catch us!"

Frank felt uncomfortable and turned away. Leopold noticed this peculiar behaviour, feeling concerned.

"Hey, are you feeling well, Frank?" he asked.

"Yes...I'm fine. I'll see you later," said Frank, walking away. He felt some guilt over his actions, but decided there was no turning back. He walked home, greeting the occasional passer-by. He finally reached the flat and entered the bedroom. Alexis was sat up in bed with a disgruntled expression reading her novel.

"Good evening. It was nice of you to turn up," she declared in a warlike mood.

"I had university matters to attend to," said Frank, defensively.

"The usual story. I can smell alcohol – you were in a bar."

"That's right."

"Where there any women involved?"

"What's that supposed to mean?"

"You heard me. Were there any women there?"

"A few."

"What were you discussing?"

"I told you, university matters. Nothing that would interest you."

"Of course not. I'm just a housewife."

"Why are you moaning? I took you out last week."

"Wow. I suppose I should be eternally grateful."

"It would help. If you like, we can go out again."

"That's better...Where can we go?"

"It's up to you. We can see a play at the theatre if you want."

"Yes, I'd like that. Now...are you coming to bed?"

"Yes, I'll be ready soon."

CHAPTER NINE

It was time for Frank's meeting with Austin so he could disclose the plans of the Democratic Party. It was the evening and the air was still, as an aeroplane flew overhead. Frank circled the fountain admiring its beauty and simplicity, wishing his own life was less complicated than it had been recently. Austin approached the fountain with an expectant expression.

"Good evening," he said.

"Austin," said Frank.

"How did the meeting go?"

"The members were discussing staging a protest march against the government."

"Where?"

"Here in Drapov. I'm sorry, I don't know the exact route."

"Who will participate in the march?"

"Students and lecturers."

"When?"

"In a few weeks time. Unfortunately, I don't have an exact date."

"Can you be more specific about the aims of the march?"

"The members want to express their views, to build support for the Democratic Party and..."

"And?"

"To overthrow the government."

"Well done. This is valuable information."

"Here are my notes."

"Thanks. The Communist Party will be grateful."

"That's good."

"Will you attend the next meeting?"

"Yes."

"Excellent."

"Will the government try to stop the march?"

"I'm not at liberty to say. But let's put it this way, we don't want to blow your cover. Still, I'll see you the same time next week?"

"Agreed."

The two men departed. Austin was happy with his conversation with Frank and looked forward to discussing his information with the Communist Party. Frank was still glad to be helping Austin and the government.

CHAPTER TEN

The time for the following meeting of the Democratic Party arose. Frank and Theodor met outside the Blue Boar, breathing the night air. They entered the establishment, hoping for a successful evening. They walked over to the bar as two mysterious men in long, dark coats observed them (through the window) from outside the building.

"Two ales, please," ordered Frank.

"Coming right up," said the young barmaid.

"Does the meeting take place here?" asked Theodor, looking around the bar.

"No, we go upstairs," said Frank.

"Right," said Theodor.

Leopold approached the two friends.

"Good evening," said Leopold.

"Leopold, this is Theodor," said Frank.

"Pleased to meet you," said Leopold, shaking Theodor's hand.

"Hi," said Theodor.

"Really, we must go upstairs now. There is a great deal to discuss," said the student.

"Of course," said Frank.

The members of the Democratic Party entered the hallway and ascended the stairs. Meanwhile, the two mysterious men walked into the establishment and approached the varnished bar. Leopold stepped over to the hallway to be followed by Frank and Leopold with their drinks. The two mysterious men ordered from the bar. In the meeting room upstairs, Hammond looked out of the window and surveyed the street below. He then viewed the room to notice Leopold, Frank and Theodor had entered.

"At last, we are all here!" said Hammond and very soon everyone was seated."We have two new people among us tonight."

"Yes. This is Reuben, an air pilot," said Melissa, excitedly.

"Good evening," said Reuben, a young man with light blue eyes and wavy brown hair. He wore a white t shirt underneath a black leather jacket, plus faded blue jeans and black boots.

"And this is Theodor, an insurance clerk," said Frank.

"Please, you don't have to show off about me," said Theodor, chuckling.

Melissa giggled and fluttered her eye lashes at the clerk, innocently.

Downstairs, the two mysterious men, in their thirties, sat at a table. One had blue eyes with fair hair, the other had brown eyes and hair. They both wore black trousers and shoes, saying little to each other. The blue eyed one nodded, stepped over to the hallway and quietly ascended the stairs, without being noticed by the bar staff. He reached the landing where he carefully listened to the conversation inside the meeting room. Inside, the discussion continued.

"..so how do you intend helping Theodor escape to Germany? He wants to live there," said Frank.

"I have a light aeroplane. I can take off from a disused airstrip near the eastern border, fly over to Germany and land in a disused airstrip I know of there," explained Reuben.

"What about radar? We don't want to be detected by the authorities," said Theodor.

"Don't worry, my friend. I'll fly low, so we can escape detection," said Reuben.

"What if we are seen by the authorities?" asked Theodor.

"I will fly in the early hours of the morning at a time when it is fairly dark. By the time we reach the border, it will be lighter," reassured Reuben.

"It sounds like a reasonable plan," said Theodor.

"There is an element of risk to what we are doing, but I like to live dangerously," said Reuben.

"Do you want payment for your services?" asked Frank.

"Yes. The escape needs some funding," said Reuben.

"We also have friends of the Democratic Party in Germany who will greet you on arrival and look after you until you are settled," said Hammond.

"That's great. Many thanks," said Theodor.

On the landing, the blue eyed mysterious man checked his watch: it was 8.20pm. He quietly descended the stairs and joined his colleague. They quickly finished their drinks, looked around, then departed from the establishment. A while later, the upstairs meeting drew to a close and the members left the Blue Boar. Some of them talked outside.

"See you, Leopold," said Frank.

"Good night," said Leopold.

Frank and Theodor began their walk home. They passed another bar with music emerging from inside. A group of teenage girls walked by, joking and giggling.

"What did you think?" asked Frank.

"It was a constructive evening and I look forward to the escape," said Theodor.

"What is your view of Reuben?"

"I have faith in him. He is a sound man and I believe he can do the job," said Theodor, grabbing his friend."This is excellent. I'll soon be out of this country and free to live my life in Germany!"

"Calm yourself, man! Don't take anything for granted.""

"Goodness! You're always so cautious."

"It's the best way."

"Well, I'm looking forward to the flight."

The two friends separated in order to return to their homes. Eventually Frank neared the entrance of the block of flats that included his. He entered, ascended the stairs and was soon inside his flat where he reflected over that night's events, hoping Theodor's escape would be successful and safe.

CHAPTER ELEVEN

Frank's latest meeting with Austin was due, so the lecturer departed from his flat one evening. He passed a neighbour, a young lady, on the landing and they greeted each other. He then descended the stairs where he crossed Marius, who was in good spirits.

"Good evening," said Marius.

"Hi," said Frank.

"What are you up to this fine evening?"

"I'm off to meet someone."

"How intriguing. Nothing dubious, I hope."

"Of course not."

"It's just that you hear stories about academics..."

"What kind of stories?"

"I'd rather not say."

"You're teasing me."

"Am I? Still, how is Alexis?"

"She is well. However, we are going through a turbulent patch."

"Take charge of the situation," demanded Marius, grabbing Frank."Alexis is a good woman – and a good cook. You mustn't lose her!"

"I'll do my best."

"Make sure you do!"

"Really, I have to go now. Goodbye."

"Look after yourself.

Marius felt troubled and watched Frank descend the stairs, then leave the building. Marius decided to follow his neighbour so he soon pursued him. Frank walked down various streets, unaware that Marius was behind him.

Frank reached Capital Park and approached the fountain. He glanced at his watch, hoping Austin would not be late. Marius hid behind some bushes, aiming to observe his neighbour without being detected. Soon enough, Austin walked up to Frank as water gently splashed in the fountain.

"Austin," said Frank, glad the wait was over.

"Frank. I trust you have more information for me. My superiors were interested in the planned demonstration you mentioned last week," said Austin, smiling.

"Indeed. I have the date and locality of the demonstration. Here is my report."

"Thank you. Is there anything else you want to tell me?"

"Like what?"

"Was anything else discussed at the meeting?"

"No. Everything you need to know is in the report."

"Very well. Will I see you next week?"

"Well…"

"Come now. The Communist Party appreciates your co-operation. The Ministry of Information values your reports. Your position at the University is secure – you know how academics who oppose the government risk becoming political prisoners."

"Are you warning me?"

"I am informing you of the status quo."

"My situation is precarious."

"By assisting the government, you gain the protection of the government."

"That is reassuring."

"And you are serving the state instead of engaging in matters of self-interest."

"That's true."

"So I'll see you next week?"

"Of course."

The two men shook hands, then departed. Marius had been listening to the conversation and he was troubled. He figured Frank had become some kind of informer for the government, but he felt uncomfortable with all this secrecy. He slowly returned home, unsure what to do.

CHAPTER TWELVE

It was the early hours of the morning and the sky was turning lighter. A small aeroplane was flying above and across the beautiful Malvarian landscape. Reuben was the pilot whilst Theodor was his passenger. The sound of the plane broke the silence of the morning sky as the sun rose in the distance.

"The border is up ahead. We are nearly there," declared Reuben.

"That's great news," said Theodor, overcome with excitement.

"Wait a minute. There's a fighter plane behind us," said Reuben, observing the aircraft from the Malvarian Air Force.

"You're kidding."

"No, it's on our tail."

"What shall we do?"

"Let's hope it's not hostile."

"What if…"

The fighter plane fired a missile which hit Reuben's aircraft and exploded. The resultant noise filled the sky. The fighter plane changed course and flew away. Theodor woke up from this dream, then sat up with a jolt. He was in his bed at home.

"No!" he cried, feeling shocked.

He looked around the bedroom, then rose from his bed and entered the hall. He walked into the bathroom, then turned on the light. He looked at himself in the mirror; his expression was at once desperate and hopeful. He poured water into his hands and threw it onto his face, trying to cool down. He dried himself, then departed from the room. He entered the bedroom and walked over to the bed. He picked up a book from the bedside table, climbed into bed, then opened the book. He looked up at the ceiling, then out of the window at the night sky, where he saw the moon.

Meanwhile, Frank was in bed at home, feeling troubled. He rose from the bed, walked over to the window and viewed the sky. Alexis was also in bed where she awoke.

"Frank, it's late," she said.

"Go back to sleep," said Frank.

"Don't tell me what to do."

"Typical."

"You've been up to something lately, I can tell."

"You're imagining things."

"You keep going out at night."

"I've told you why."

"There's something on your mind."

"It's nothing."

Alexis arose from the bed, then stepped over to Frank. She was determined to acquire the truth from Frank about his recent mood and behaviour. She looked at him with a serious, concerned expression.

"Are you seeing another woman?" she asked.

"Don't be ridiculous," said Frank, feeling annoyed.

"Deny it!"

"Get a grip, woman."

"You take me for granted!"

"If only you knew."

"Tell me what's going on or I'm leaving!"

Frank paused, then spoke:"I'm helping Theodor escape to Germany."

"That's illegal," said Alexis.

"It's what he wants."

"It's dangerous."

"He's a friend."

"Frank, you are a brave man. You are a good man," she hugged him."I'm sorry I shouted at you. I didn't realise."

"I want Theodor to be happy so I'm going to help him to escape."

"I understand," said Alexis, returning to bed.

"Sure, I'll be with you in a minute," said Frank. He viewed the sky once more, then soon slipped into bed. He was glad to have cleared the air with Alexis and viewed the future with some intrepidity, hoping Thoedor's escape would be successful.

CHAPTER THIRTEEN

A few days later, Frank purchased a newspaper from a newsagent, then strolled over to Capital Park, where he sat on a vacant bench. It was a sunny day with a few clouds floating in the sky. Some cyclists passed Frank, enjoying their leisure time as Frank read the paper. Marius was walking nearby by coincidence, then spotted the lecturer and recalled his encounter with Austin. Marius had a troubled expression as he approached the lecturer.

"Frank," said Marius, rubbing his chin, which indicated his disquiet.

"Marius! Are you following me?" asked Frank, quite surprised by the presence of his neighbour.

"No, of course not."

"I'm glad to hear it. Are you going to sit down? You might get hit by one of these crazy cyclists."

A few of them passed by, then Marius sat down. The sun hid behind a cloud and Frank put down the paper. He sensed his neighbour had a problem.

"What's the matter? Your expression says something is bothering you," said the lecturer.

"Well..." started Marius, briefly looking at his shoes.

"What's up? Are you having a secret love affair with an impressionable young girl?"

"No, not at all. It's just that...I suspect someone I know is an informer."

"An informer? How do you mean?"

"I suspect he is providing the Secret Police with information."

"Who is this person?"

"No one you know."

"Why are you telling me?"

"I thought you might give me some advice."

"It may be best to keep quiet about this matter. It is dangerous to interfere with this type of thing. Understand?"

"Yes."

"I suggest you enjoy your retirement in peace."

"I bid you farewell. I have other matters to attend to," said Marius, standing up.

"Goodbye," said Frank, picking up his paper once more.

Marius walked away, still feeling uneasy. He thought Frank might have confessed to being an informer and had not anticipated this level of opposition. Marius was uncertain about this situation: he did not want to land himself in trouble, but was perplexed over Frank assisting the Secret Police.

CHAPTER FOURTEEN

It was the early morning outside the block of flats where Frank and Alexis resided. The couple stood here and saw a car up ahead, which was driven by Hammond. Reuben sat next to him, with Theodor and Melissa in the back. The car was a blue saloon, which soon parked outside the flats.

"Here they are," said Frank, as Hammond lowered his door window.

"Good morning," said the driver.

"Hi. This is Alexis, my other half," said Frank.

"Pleased to meet you. The weather is good for the flight," commented Alexis, looking up at the sky.

"I agree," said Hammond, smiling.

"Good luck, Theodor," said Alexis.

"Thank you. Why don't you come with me?" asked Theodor, cheekily.

"It's very tempting," joked Alexis.

"She's better off with me," said Frank, amused.

Frank entered the back of the car, where he sat next to Melissa.

"Is everybody set?" inquired Hammond, glancing into the rear view mirror.

"Yes. Carry on," requested Frank.

"Goodbye," said Hammond, starting the car.

"See you," said Alexis, waving and hoping Theodor would not encounter any difficulties during his escape.

The car drove off as Alexis noticed a curtain move inside one of the flats. She felt rather vexed about this for the escape was supposed to be secret. She soon entered the building, but did not investigate the moving curtain further.

The blue car sped across Drapov for there was little traffic at that time of the morning. The driver and passengers were rather nervous, but excited as well. Melissa was pleased to be part of this ambitious venture.

"I'm so excited!" she exclaimed.

"Cool it. We haven't reached the runway yet," said Reuben, trying to calm her.

"It's an adventure," declared Melissa.

"It won't be so much fun if we get caught," remarked Hammond, aware of the hazardous nature of their escapade.

"Don't say that!" asked Melissa.

"Don't develop a false sense of security," requested Hammond.

"Typical! Lecturers – you're always lecturing!" said Melissa, feeling frustrated.

"That's their job!" said Theodor.

"What do you know about education?" asked Frank.

"Very little. I left school as soon as possible," said Theodor.

"It shows!" remarked Frank.

"What will you do in Germany?" asked Melissa.

"I will get a job as an insurance clerk. It's all I know," said Theodor.

Hammond continued driving the car as the passengers conversed inside. Soon they reached the beautiful countryside, away from the noise and pollution of the city. Hammond drove past a field dotted with poppies.

"Is it much further?" asked Theodor, feeling rather impatient

"We're nearly there," said Reuben.

"Wait a minute. There's a car behind us," remarked Melissa.

It was a black and white police car. The lights started to flash and the siren wailed like the voice of doom. The people inside the blue car felt anxious.

"Damn," said Hammond, fearing Theodor's escape could be over.

"Don't panic," said Frank, trying to be optimistic.

Hammond stopped his car and parked by the side of the road. The other car slowed down, then parked behind the blue one. A police officer stepped out and approached Hammond and the others. The officer viewed the blue car with his observant blue eyes, then scratched his short, brown hair, apparently puzzled by the sight before him. Hammond wound down his window, feeling uneasy.

"Good morning," said the police officer, scanning Hammond and the passengers with an air of suspicion.

"Good morning, officer," said Hammond, gulping.

"Tell me, where are you heading at this time of the morning? You should be in bed."

"We're off to visit some friends in a town nearby. We're travelling in order to avoid the traffic."

"I see. Still, show me your driver's license."

Hammond handed it over to be checked by the officer, who said:"Everything seems to be in order. Now this was just a routine check so you are free to go."

"Thank you, officer," said Hammond, feeling relieved.

The police officer returned to his car, smirking. The people in the blue car looked at each other for support. Meanwhile, a farmer drove past in a rusty old tractor.

"Thank God the police man didn't question us further. I'm not a good liar," said Melissa.

Hammond drove off. Soon the blue car reached the entrance to the airstrip. There was no one around, which was reassuring.

"At last," said Melissa, feeling relieved and excited.

Hammond drove into the airstrip and continued until he reached an area near the runway. He parked near to a light aeroplane, allowing everyone to depart from the car. Everybody stretched their legs and viewed the environment. Reuben admired the aeroplane.

"There she is," he said, chuckling.

"Excellent," said Theodor, regarding his means of escape to a new life.

"I will open the boot to retrieve your luggage," said Hammond, stepping over to the car. He removed the luggage from the boot, then handed them over to Theodor. "Here you are, then."

"Thank you," said Theodor, receiving the two bags.

Everyone walked over to the aeroplane. Reuben opened the door to enter. Melissa hugged Theodor, feeling strong emotions.

"Good luck," she said.

Frank hugged Theodor, both friends knowing they may not see each other again.

"I will be thinking of you," said Frank.

Hammond hugged Theodor.

"I hope we meet again under different circumstances," said Hammond.

Three identical, black cars drove towards the aeroplane. Their arrival was ominous. They slowed down and parked nearby.

"Hang on a minute. Who is this?" asked Melissa, fearing the escape was over.

Two men in dark, long coats emerged from each car. Their appearance was serious and menacing. Two of them were the mysterious ones at the Blue Boar.

"Hell. It's the Secret Police," said Hammond.

"Damn. I'm too young to die," said Melissa.

"Don't panic," urged Frank.

"This is all my fault," said Theodor, regretfully.

"I am Detective Joseph Pulnik from the Secret Service. You are all under arrest for assisting an unauthorised emigration," he said, authoritatively. He presented his identification badge to the gathering. He wore spectacles and possessed blue eyes with short, fair hair. He was tall and around forty.

"Who tipped you off," asked Theodor, angrily.

"You have the right to remain silent and anything you say may be used against you," stated Detective Pulnik in a clinical manner.

Each person in the group was arrested and handcuffed to their dismay. They were led to the black cars under an atmosphere of foreboding. Their hopes had been dashed.

"Where are you taking us?" inquired Hammond, urgently.

"To Headquarters," said Detective Pulnik, decisively.

The group were guided into the black cars, looking gloomy and rather anxious. They were followed into the cars by the Secret Service Agents, who were serious and business like. The cars drove off and eventually arrived at the Secret Service Headquarters, an official looking building in Drapov. The group were taken to the foyer then put into a grey cell.

"They can't treat us like this," asserted Melissa, feeling like a caged animal.

"They can and they are," replied Hammond, feeling frustrated.

"The bastards!" exclaimed Melissa.

"They will release us," said Frank.

"How do you know?" asked Reuben, suspiciously.

"Do you know something we don't?" asked Theodor, applying some pressure.

A young Secret Service Agent approached the cell to be noticed by the group. He seemed to find the scene amusing and even smiled, like a lion snarling at its prey. He opened the door causing a harsh, metallic sound to echo around the cell.

"Frank Vockins is wanted for questioning," he said, bluntly.

"That's me," said Frank.

"When are you going to let us out of here?" implored Melissa.

"Patience, young lady. Come on," said the Agent, gruffly, guiding Frank out of the cell.

The Agent locked the cell door, leaving its occupants to ponder their future. He accompanied Frank down a corridor until they arrived at a dark grey door. There was an eerie atmosphere in the building.

"A detective wishes to speak with you. Be polite," requested the Agent with a menacing smile.

They entered the office where they saw a window, filing cabinets, a few chairs and pictures on the walls. There was a large, varnished table near the centre of the office. Someone sat behind it facing the back wall. He spun around in a manner that appeared theatrical to Frank as it was a dramatic gesture.

"You?" blurted Frank, surprised by the presence before him.

"Yes," said Austin in a welcoming manner.

"You organised this?"

"I'm the one who asks the questions."

"How did you find out about…"

"About your attempt to assist an unauthorised emigration? Walls have ears."

The young Agent sniggered and Frank glared at him.

"Sit down," ordered Austin, waving his hand at a chair.

"I'd rather stand," said Frank, defiantly.

"Sit down," reiterated Austin, looking at the Agent.

Frank sat down.

"The government frowns upon unauthorised emigration," continued Austin, squinting at the lecturer.

"I was helping a friend," replied Frank.

"Your loyalty should be towards the state."

"I'm human."

"Political ideology should displace selfish motives."

"You talk about morality? I feel betrayed."

"You are an informer. You have betrayed your colleagues."

"You and I had an agreement. I provide you with information in order to assist the Communist Party."

"That is right."

"And you reward me by arresting me."

"Relax, Frank...You and your colleagues will be released."

"Without charge?"

"Yes, provided our agreement continues."

Frank nodded.

"I will see you at the same time, same place?" asked Austin.

Frank nodded.

"Have you anymore to say? Do you have more information for me before our next meeting?" inquired Austin.

"No," said Frank.

"Does anyone suspect you of being an informer?"

"No, not as far as I know."

"That's good."

Meanwhile, back in the cell, the occupants were troubled and looked haggard. They disliked being locked up in a grim environment and longed for their liberty. They wondered what the future held for them.

"I wonder what they are discussing," said Reuben, wringing his hands.

"Us," said Theodor, raising his arms.

"Why did they choose to question Frank?" asked Reuben, feeling puzzled.

"I don't know," said Theodor.

"I'm not sure about Frank," said Reuben.

"What are you trying to say?" asked Hammond, feeling rather alarmed.

"Maybe they know him," suggested Reuben, who stood up from the bench. "Maybe he is an informer."

"Don't be ridiculous! He is a friend of mine," retorted Theodor, baffled by this suggestion.

"What proof do you have?" asked Hammond, standing up as well.

"I have no proof," replied Reuben, shrugging his shoulders.

"Why would he inform on us and get himself arrested?" asked Melissa, feeling vexed.

"Look, I don't have all the answers, but I am suspicious," continued Reuben, walking around the cell.

"Frank is a man of sound character. He would not betray us," proposed Theodor, feeling a need to defend his friend.

"He is a respected academic," said Hammond, rubbing his chin.

"Are you going to challenge him?" asked Melissa, starting to enjoy the conflict.

"This is the Democratic Party! We should all challenge him – or elect someone to challenge him," argued Reuben, emphatically.

"Keep your voice down, man. Remember where we are," said Hammond, attempting to maintain order and fairness.

"You worry too much. Still, I'm sick of this place. I feel like an animal trapped inside a cage," said Reuben, kicking the bars aggressively.

"Be careful," said Melissa.

"I think we should have evidence before we challenge Frank," proposed Hammond, tentatively.

"How do we gather evidence? Hire a private detective?" asked Reuben.

"What do you suggest we do, then?" asked Hammond.

"I say we confront him and ask him if he's an informer," said Reuben, firmly.

"He would find that offensive," said Theodor, thinking of his friend's sensibility.

"This isn't a dinner party. Our future and the future of the country is at stake. What have manners got to do with it?" asked Reuben.

"Look, let's keep an eye on him for the time being," suggested Hammond.

"If we ever see him or daylight again," said Reuben.

"Don't talk like that," said Melissa.

Frank approached the cell with the young Agent. Frank was relieved his meeting with Austin was over and that they were all going to be released. He viewed his colleagues in the cell, then wondered if they had been discussing him.

"Speak of the devil," said Reuben.

"Hush," said Hammond.

The young Agent opened the cell door.

"Where have you been? We thought you'd eloped," declared Theodor.

"I've been talking with a detective. We are free to go," said Frank, smiling.

"Fantastic!" said Melissa, looking forward to returning home.

"How did you persuade him to release us?" asked Reuben with an air of suspicion.

"He decided the offence wasn't too serious," confirmed Frank.

"Well done," said Theodor, pleased with his friend.

"So, he has dropped the charges?" inquired Hammond.

"Yes. The slate is clean.

"Is everyone ready to leave? If you want to, you can stay," said the young Agent, sarcastically.

"Let's go," said Frank.

"What a shame. This place could benefit from having a pretty lady around," said the Agent, admiring Melissa's appearance.

Melissa felt self-conscious and grimaced. The Agent led everyone out of the cell. The group relished their rediscovered freedom and were soon standing outside the building. Hammond, Theodor and Frank entered the back of a black car, whilst Melissa along with Reuben entered the back of another one. There were two Agents in the front of each car. After a short while, the cars drove off and travelled down the streets of Drapov. The first car stopped outside the block of flats where Frank lived. He departed from the vehicle, glad to be home.

"Remember, no more funny business," said an Agent with a menacing glance.

"I'll catch you later," said Theodor.

"Bye now," said Frank, as the car sped off.

Frank watched the car until it turned around a corner. He then faced the entrance to the flats and looked upwards. He reflected upon his recent experiences, but resolved to remain loyal to the Communist Party. He walked through the entrance with an earnest expression.

The scene was Capital Square in bright daytime. Hundreds of students along with academics were marching forward, carrying banners proclaiming DEMOCRACY NOW, DOWN WITH THE GOVERNMENT, POWER TO THE PEOPLE, END COMMUNIST RULE and so on. Hammond was at the front of the march, feeling invigorated. He declared:"Our time has come!"

The protestors met a wall of riot police. Here there was a tense atmosphere. Without warning, a student launched a projectile at the police, which led them to attack the protestors.

Frank opened his eyes to awake from the dream. He sat up in his bed at home. Next to him, Alexis woke up too.

"What's the matter?" she asked, squinting with tired eyes.

"I – I had a dream, that's all," replied Frank.

"Go back to sleep."

Frank lay back and looked out of the window at the night sky. The half moon was visible, plus the sound of late night revellers could be heard as they returned home after an evening out. Frank closed his eyes to consider the meaning of his dream.

CHAPTER FIFTEEN

It was the evening at the university in Room 12, which was in the History Faculty. Hammond, Sabrina, Stefan, Frank, Leopold, Melissa, Theodor and some other people were gathered here. Krystof, a mature student with green eyes and black hair, attended this time. He was dressed in black with a leather jacket, plain t-shirt, straight jeans and boots. Hammond sat behind a table, whilst everyone sat facing him.

"Right everyone, we are meeting here because I feel it is not safe to meet in the Blue Boar any longer since our brush with the Secret Police. It seems someone was listening in on our conversation and knew of our plan to help Theodor escape to Germany," explained Hammond.

Reuben looked at Frank suspiciously. Frank did not notice this, but was rather concerned that his cover could be blown and the others could discover he was an informer. As a result, he felt uncomfortable.

"To continue, it is likely the government knows of the existence of the Democratic Party, but it is up to us to continue in our aim to bring democracy to Malvaria," said Hammond.

"Here! Here!" cheered Melissa, banging the table with her fist.

"Our plan is to hold a prodemocracy demonstration in Capital Square next month. We will express our opposition to the government and will demand democratic elections in order to acquire freedom and achieve self determination."

"I think we should ask the authorities for permission for the demonstration," proposed Frank.

"Don't be ridiculous. They wouldn't allow it," said Reuben.

"How do you know?"

"Sorry. I forgot how friendly you are with the government."

"What's that supposed to mean?"

"You're the one who spoke to the Secret Police detective and got us released…"

"Would you rather still be in the cell?"

"I'm only saying…"

"Be careful of what you say."

"Or else?"

"Gentlemen, calm yourselves! We are civilised people," urged Hammond.

"We are democratic people, we are allowed to differ," said Reuben.

"I want everyone to trust me on this matter. If we hold a demonstration without permission, the police could arrive and disband us. It pays to be cautious," suggested Frank.

"But we can't trust the government. It always has the upper hand," said Reuben.

"What does everyone else think?" asked Frank, opening up the debate.

"Frank has made a strong case," said Melissa.

"Why don't we vote on the matter?" asked Hammond.

"Yes, let's have a vote!" agreed Leopold, feeling energised.

"Everyone who believes we should inform the authorities about our demonstration, raise your arm," instructed Hammond, observing everyone.

Most people raised their arm to Reuben's annoyance. Frank was pleased that he had won the argument. However, Melissa was worried about the tempestuous pilot!

"And those people who disagree, raise your arm, " said Hammond.

Reuben raised his arm, clearly angry that no one else had raised their's.

"It is clear most people believe we should inform the authorities about our demo," said Hammond.

Reuben walked out of the room, displeased with the result of the vote. Melissa looked alarmed and felt worried about the mental state of her boyfriend. She quickly stood up.

"Reuben!" she cried and chased after him.

"I wish I had that effect on women," said Hammond, watching Melissa leave the room."Indeed, Frank, it is evident you have won the argument."

"Reuben is a fiery young man, but I'm confident I'm right about this matter. I will contact the government and inform you of their decision."

Krystof regarded Frank suspiciously as though he was displeased about the lecturer's relationship with the government. In a corridor, Melissa briskly pursued Reuben and managed to reach him. She was out of breath.

"Reuben! Stop!" she cried, grabbing the pilot.

"Let go!" Reuben demanded.

"No!" retorted Melissa, as the couple stopped."What's the matter with you?"

"That man is bad news!"

"That's not what the others think."

"He's an informer, a collaborator!"

"You have no proof of that."

"He knows how the government thinks."

"He's a smart man."

"You are naive."

"You need to deal with life's uncertainties without becoming hysterical. Come to the next meeting to find out if the authorities will allow the demonstration."

Reuben walked off to be watched by Melissa. She hoped he would calm down and that Frank was not an informer. However, she suspected Frank could be assisting the Secret Police owing to his support of communism.

CHAPTER SIXTEEN

It was the evening in Capital Park. Here Austin stood by the fountain, the traditional meeting place for him and Frank. The Detective felt impatient as he was keen to hear the latest news from the lecturer. Soon, Frank arrived.

"You are late," said Austin, tapping the face of his expensive watch.

"Better late than never," said Frank, shrugging his shoulders.

"Time is of the essence. What is the latest?"

"I told the Democratic Party I would inform the authorities of the demonstration they intend holding."

"What was the reaction?"

"Most of the members approved of my intention. However, it seems one of them suspects me of being an informer."

"How come?"

"He says I am friendly with the government."

"Does he have proof you are an informer?"

"No."

"What do the other members think?"

"I suspect they are undecided."

"Perhaps we should terminate your role. It would be dangerous if they all suspect you of being an informer – or find out that you are one."

"But I have enjoyed my role. I want to find out what the Democratic Party is going to do next."

"Do you think you will be safe if you attend the next meeting?"

"Yes, I do."

"In that case, attend the next one and we will review your role when we meet again."

"What about the demonstration? Will your superiors in the Communist Party allow it to take place?"

"When is the proposed date of the demonstration?"

"This coming Saturday."

"I will ask them and inform you of their decision. I have your 'phone number in my notes."

"Talking of notes, here are mine."

"Thank you."

The two men departed, concerned with the significant changes that were occurring in their country. The next day, Austin rang Frank with the Communist Party's decision: the demonstration would be allowed to take place. The lecturer had mixed feelings about this and wondered if political change was of long term benefit to the country.

CHAPTER SEVENTEEN

It was the evening at the University. The Democratic Party gathered for an important meeting in Room 12 once more. There was a buzz of excitement as the members wondered if the demonstration would take place. Hammond sat at a desk facing everyone, hoping the evening would be fruitful.

"Good evening everyone. It is time to ask Frank if he has gained permission from the authorities for us to hold our demonstration in Capital Square on Saturday," said Hammond.

"The good news is that the government have given us permission to hold the demo. They are not as harsh as they once were," announced Frank.

"Indeed, this is good news, excellent news," remarked Hammond.

"But where is Reuben?" asked Frank.

"He could not come tonight. He has stomach ache," said Melissa.

"That is a shame. To continue, I was informed there will be a police presence at the demo in order to maintain order."

"But we must still deliver our message – our demand for democracy," said Melissa.

"Of course," reassured Hammond.

The Party continued to discuss and plan the demonstration in an optimistic mood. Hope was in the air with everyone looking forward to the future. Eventually, the meeting drew to a close and the members returned home.

CHAPTER EIGHTEEN

It was the afternoon at Frank's flat during a warm, sunny day. Frank was standing on the balcony, watching the street activities below. A bus passed by and some school children crossed the road. The lecturer entered the living room. Here Alexis was reading a magazine on the sofa.

"I want to go shopping tomorrow," she said, not looking up.

"I'm sorry, I can't go with you," disclosed Frank.

"There's no such word as 'can't'," said Alexis, looking up this time.

"There's something I have to tell you," said Frank, sitting next to her.

Alexis paused, feeling bemused, then spoke:"Let me guess – you're having a sex change, you're pregnant, the world is going to end yesterday?"

"No, I'm going to a political demonstration at Capital Square tomorrow.

"In aid of what?"

"The democratic Party is holding the rally to demand democratic elections."

"Has the government allowed it?"

"Yes."

"Will you be safe?"

"Yes, I should be."

"How long have you been involved with the Democratic Party?"

"The past few months…"

"Wait a second. That's where you've been all those evenings…"

"You're right, I've been attending the meetings."

"Why didn't you tell me?"

"It wasn't safe to tell you. The Democratic Party tried to help Theodor escape to Germany."

"This relationship can't survive with all these secrets."

"I have told you the truth now."

"What else are you hiding?"

"Nothing more."

"There had better be no more skeletons in the closet – or I'm off!"

"Where are you going?"

"To see a friend and save my sanity."

Alexis entered the hall ,then left the flat. Frank felt frustrated and kicked the wall. He hoped Alexis would forgive him for keeping secrets from her.

CHAPTER NINETEEN

It was the day of the political demonstration. The street leading to Capital Square was full of students and lecturers marching onwards. They held banners with the following messages: 'DEMOCRATIC ELECTIONS NOW', 'DEMOCRACY FOR THE PEOPLE', 'DOWN WITH THE COMMUNISTS' and so on. Frank marched with Hammond to show his apparent support for the Democratic Party. The protestors chanted:"What do we want? Democracy! When do we want it? Now!" Many members of the public watched the march, hoping that change was in the air. A significant number of policemen observed the proceedings.

"Our time has come!" said Hammond to Frank, feeling jubilant and impressed by the turn out.

Alexis stood on the pavement as the protestors passed. She and Frank saw each other, both wondering what the future held for their relationship and their country. However, their emotions were stirred by the excitement and optimism of the march. The protestors reached the Square, then moved towards a podium. Here, Hammond ascended the stairs until he reached the top of it. During his ascent, the protestors cheered, overcome with fervour. He addressed them with a clear, strong voice befitting the occasion:"Students and fellow lecturers, we have gathered here today to vocalize our demands. The people of Malvaria have lived for a long time under communist rule, but the time has come for change. I and other members of the Democratic Party demand democratic elections so the people can decide who governs them. Give the people the vote so the people can choose their government. The time has come to overthrow tyranny and establish democracy. The time has come to grant the people civil rights and to elect the

Democratic Party. What we demand are free and fair elections so that power can be given back to the people."

The policemen appeared to be uneasy, as though Hammond's revolutionary words disturbed them. Austin was in the crowd observing the demonstration, apparently unhappy but alert. He and Frank noticed each other, the latter felt tense as well as uncertain. Reuben saw these two men and the pilot felt unsettled, even angry. Hammond gauged the mood of the crowd, sensing their desire for a better future. He continued his important speech:"For too long we have lived in fear, for too long we have lived under political oppression, but now is the time to demand the freedom of speech and to fight for our rights. We demand the release of political prisoners whose only crime is to oppose the government. We demand the release of writers and academics imprisoned by the communists. For too long the communist leaders have stifled political dissent, but now the time has come to stand up and speak out. This country is prosperous, but it is also oppressive. It is time to speak out and end this oppression."

Austin was displeased with Hammond's rhetoric. He nodded at three policemen who ascended the podium. They approached Hammond, who looked alarmed.

"What is going on here? What do you want?" asked Hammond.

"You have said enough today. It is time to end the demonstration," said a policeman, named Detective Dolan.

"But I haven't finished," protested Hammond.

"You are under arrest," said Detective Dolan, putting handcuffs onto the lecturer.

Stefan was on the podium and he was incensed by these events. He walked over to Detective Dolan to voice his concerns. The atmosphere was tense and foreboding.

"Hey! What are you playing at? This demonstration was been authorised by the government!" declared Stefan, bravely.

"Arrest him," said Detective Dolan and one of the other policemen put handcuffs on the student.

"This is an outrage!" said Stefan, defiantly.

The crowd opposed these arrests so they booed and moved forward. Austin was concerned about this so he spoke on his walkie talkie, then walked away from the crowd. Soon four police vans arrived on the scene and a potent number of riot police descended from them. With their visors down plus their shields up, they waded into the crowd, waving their truncheons, thereby causing panic and alarm. The three policemen on the podium led Hammond and Stefan down the steps, then into a nearby police van. Frank managed to reach the podium, where he met Sabrina. The scene was chaotic and distressing as the riot police attempted to disperse the crowd.

"Frank! What can we do?" asked Sabrina, feeling alarmed as she watched these events unfold.

"Hammond and Stefan will be taken to the police station. We'll have to go there," replied Frank, concerned about his colleagues' welfare. He had some knowledge of police procedure.

The van containing Hammond and Stefan drove off, away from the mayhem. Austin observed this so he entered the back of a black car, which followed the van. Meanwhile, the riot police beat some of the protestors and rounded up others, pushing them into the back of available police vans. Frank saw this behaviour, which he found appalling. Sabrina was horrified too.

"My car is parked nearby. I'll drive us to the station," said Sabrina.

Melissa and Hugh joined the two lecturers. They were all shocked by the violence around them. A few trouble makers threw bricks at the police, increasing the turmoil.

"This is terrible!" shouted Melissa, feeling outraged.

"This is history!" declared Hugh, apparently moved by the disturbances.

"Sabrina will drive us to the police station so we can negotiate the release of Hammond and Stefan!" explained Frank.

"Thank God!" said Melissa.

"That's a good idea" said Hugh.

"You had better stay behind, Hugh. We will need room in the car for our two colleagues," said Frank.

"Sure," agreed Hugh. He soon departed.

"Come on! Let's go!" urged Frank.

Sabrina led Frank and Melissa away from the podium towards her car. A misdirected brick nearly hit Frank. Reuben strode towards the trio. He was livid about the surrounding chaos.

"Where are you going?" he asked, glaring at them.

"We're going to the police station to negotiate the release of Hammond and Stefan," explained Melissa, concerned about Reuben's emotional state.

"I want to come!" he blurted, raising his arms.

"You're not coming. You're too fired up!" asserted Frank with a serious expression.

"Damn you!" retorted Reuben.

"Go home, Reuben. You'll be safe there," said Sabrina, firmly.

"Be patient. I'll call you," reassured Melissa, touching her boyfriend's cheek, then she kissed him.

Reuben walked off in a mood. Melissa hoped he would calm down soon, then turned to face Frank and Sabrina. Meanwhile, most of the crowd had dispersed.

"What a tempestuous young man!" declared Sabrina.

"Hurry! There's no time to waste," said Frank.

The trio managed to leave Capital Square relatively unscathed. Behind them, two policemen wrestled a protestor to the ground. Sabrina led Frank plus Melissa to a side street where they reached her car.

"This is much more exciting than lectures!" said Melissa.

"How would you know? You hardly ever attend lectures!" said Sabrina.

"Sabrina, there's more to education than lectures. Still, I wonder if the police have roughed up Hammond and Stefan," said Melissa.

"I hope not," said Stefan.

Once the trio were inside the car Sabrina drove off. The car travelled down various streets on its way to the police station. A short while later it arrived at the destination. Sabrina parked the car and everyone departed, then approached the station.

"I hope this doesn't take long," said Frank, bravely facing the task ahead.

"We're right behind you," said Sabrina, offering moral support.

They ascended some stone steps, then entered the station through the main doors. Sergeant Hornick was at the reception so the trio walked up to him. He was about thirty with blue eyes plus black short hair. This area was busy and bustling with noise.

"Good afternoon. Can I help?" asked the Sergeant.

"Yes. We were at the political demonstration at Capital Square earlier today. The police broke up the demo and two men, Hammond Martinek and Stefan Doubek were arrested and, we believe, taken here," said Frank.

"That is correct. The two men you mentioned have been locked up in the cell. Detective Dolan brought them in," said Sergeant Hornick as the Detective walked past.

"Good afternoon, gentlemen. Is there a problem?" asked Detective Dolan, halting for a while.

"Yes, we've come to negotiate the release of Hammond Martinek and Stefan Doubek. They were arrested today at the political demonstration," said Frank.

"They have done nothing wrong. You must release them!" demanded Melissa.

"Indeed. Would you like to follow me into my office?" asked Detective Dolan.

"Of course," said Sabrina.

The Detective led the trio down a corridor. They passed by a few policemen on their way and noticed some pictures on the walls. They reached the Detective's office, which they entered. Here, there was a polished wooden desk, some chairs, as well as filing cabinets plus diagrams on the walls. A man stood regarding a map of Drapov hanging on the wall. He swiftly turned around: it was Austin. Frank was startled by his presence.

"You? What are you doing here?" asked Frank.

"Don't act so surprised. A political demonstration is a concern for the security of the government and therefore a concern for the Secret Service," said Austin.

"You know this man?" Sabrina asked Frank.

"Yes, we met when Frank and his colleagues attempted to orchestrate the escape of a citizen to Western Europe," disclosed Austin.

"When are you going to release Hammond and Stefan?" asked Melissa.

"You have spirit, young lady. I always say a little spirit goes a long way," remarked Austin.

"Stop playing with words," said Melissa.

"But there is a spirit of change in the air. We've had reports coming in of political demonstrations occurring in cities across Malvaria. It seems the days of the Communist government are numbered," continued Austin.

"That's fantastic," said Sabrina.

"And in a democratic society, there will be no call for the Secret Police, as we are known. I'll have to look for another job," said Austin, walking over to a window.

"What about Hammond and Stefan?"

"Patience, young lady," said Austin, smiling.

"I have been patient," said Melissa.

"I will release them from the cells. They haven't been charged," said Detective Dolan.

"Why were they arrested in the first place?" asked Frank.

"Hammond was making inflammatory remarks about the government," said Austin.

"He was telling the truth, God damn it!" asserted Sabrina.

"My loyalty lies with the Communist Party," said Austin.

"And our loyalty is with the people!" said Sabrina.

"Why did the riot police attack the crowd?" asked Melissa.

"The riot police dispersed the crowd because they were disturbing the peace and represented a threat to social order," said Austin.

"You lying bastard!" said Melissa.

"There's no need to use language like that. Do you want to see your colleagues again?" asked Austin, menacingly.

"Don't threaten us!" said Melissa.

"I don't threaten people. I issue warnings," claimed Austin.

"Calm down, Melissa. We're here to negotiate, not start World War Three," said Frank, putting his hand on Melissa's shoulder.

"Don't worry, Austin is only playing with you, I will fetch your two colleagues. Please, wait at reception," said Detective Dolan, opening the door.

Frank, Sabrina and Melissa left the office, then walked over to the reception. A short while later, their two colleagues arrived with Detective Dolan. It was a happy reunion.

"How are you?" asked Frank, feeling relieved.

"I've felt better," sighed Hammond, glad to have been released.

"How have you been treated?" asked Sabrina.

"Not too badly. Don't worry about it," said Stefan, not wanting to make a fuss.

"Protests have spread to other cities," said Melissa.

"Really? That's brilliant!" said Hammond, optimistically.

"We've started the ball rolling!" said Stefan, an advocate of social change.

"There's a democratic revolution going on!" declared Melissa.

"Hey! Let's get out of here. We can go to a cafe and watch the news on TV," suggested Frank, helpfully.

"That's a good idea," said Melissa, wanting to update her knowledge of recent events.

Frank and the others left the police station, then headed towards Sabrina's car. Once inside, Sabrina drove to a cafe she liked and everyone entered. Frank approached the bar.

"Five coffees, please," he said to the barman.

"Coming right up," said the barman.

There was a TV on the wall broadcasting news about protests across Malvaria. Frank and his colleagues watched this with interest. A young, female journalist spoke: "Today's prodemocracy march ended in Capital Square where there was a political rally calling for the end of Communist rule. Thousands of people attended the march which was organised by the Democratic Party. The leader of the Democratic Party, Hammond Martinek, gave a bold and stirring speech, but was soon arrested by the police and removed from the scene. The riot police then dispersed the crowd. News of the rally spread across Malvaria and further prodemocracy demonstrations have taken place in other cities. The Communist Party is in turmoil and is now holding a crisis meeting."

"This is wonderful! I can't believe it's happening!" cried Melissa, jumping up and down.

"Here are your coffees," said the barman.

"Thank you," said Frank.

"What do we do next?" asked Sabrina.

"We must hold a meeting of the Democratic Party and discuss our plans for the future," said Hammond.

"What about the communists?" inquired Stefan.

"At some point we will have to meet them and inform them of the reforms we want," replied Hammond.

Frank and his colleagues drank their coffees and discussed the current situation. Hammond organised a meeting for the Democratic Party at the University later that day. The meeting was held in Room 12 there and the members of the Party attended.

"Good afternoon, everyone. I'm glad you could all make it here today. As we all know, momentous events have occurred recently affecting the political situation in Malvaria. The prodemocracy demonstration in Capital Square was a great success – it inspired people in other cities to protest against the government. However, the police were heavy handed with the crowd and Stefan and I were arrested and taken to a police cell."

"You were soon released," said Reuben.

"That's right. Frank, Sabrina and Melissa negotiated our release," said Hammond.

"Well, of course, Frank arranged your release. He's a great friend of the government," said Reuben.

"What are you trying to say?" asked Hammond.

"I suspect Frank of being a collaborator. We all know of them," said Reuben, defiantly.

"You're being paranoid. You have no proof," said Hammond in an attempt to defend Frank.

"The proof is waiting to be uncovered. Go on, Frank, deny my accusations," challenged Reuben, provocatively.

Frank had a troubled expression and reluctantly stood up. He had deceived his colleagues all this time, but no longer wanted to continue the masquerade. He cleared his throat and viewed the members of the Party.

"It is true, I'm afraid. I have been an informer for the Secret Police as they are known since I began attending meetings of the Democratic Party," said Frank.

Everyone was stunned. The atmosphere in the room completely changed and feelings were intense, but confused. Frank faced the music.

"Frank!" blurted Hammond, his eyes wide open.

"You see? What did I say?" asked Reuben, triumphantly.

"How could you?" demanded Hammond, flexing his authority.

"I was approached by a detective in the Secret Police some time ago. I have spied on the Democratic Party and provided him with information about the Party's plans and activities," confessed Frank, feeling the pressure."I apologise for my actions...and will cease attending meetings. I feel guilty for my behaviour and can no longer deceive you."

"This is shocking news," said Hammond.

"Don't be too harsh on Frank," said Melissa, standing up.

"Melissa, this is not a trivial matter," said Hammond.

"But look at the bigger picture: all he did was provide the Secret Police with information – no lives have been lost – and we are currently experiencing a revolution! It looks like the Communist Party will be defeated and we will soon be enjoying the freedoms of the West."

"He betrayed us," said Reuben.

"The man's character is in doubt," said Hammond.

"What is all this talk about morality? People do what they want to!" said Melissa.

"It is evident we cannot trust the man. He has let us down," said Hammond.

"Everyone deserves a second chance!" said Melissa.

"Don't worry about me," said Frank, then he left the room.

Hammond paused to collect his thoughts, then spoke:"I think we should continue the meeting. You can discuss Frank's actions later on amongst yourselves...Next week I will be meeting the leader of the Communist Party in order to discuss our demands for political reform."

"Marvellous," said Sabrina, feeling excited.

"I hope it will be a fruitful encounter," said Hammond.

The meeting continued in earnest. Hammond outlined his plans for the future and an optimistic mood returned to the room. After the meeting ended, everyone continued with their affairs.

CHAPTER TWENTY

Two girls were riding their bicycles in Capital Square. They passed Frank, who was walking along with his hands in his pockets, looking down and feeling glum owing to his earlier confession. By chance, Theodor was in the Square, feeling happy. He approached his friend in a quirky mood.

"Hey, Frank!" said Theodor, pleased to meet his friend.

"Sorry?" asked Frank, rather dazed.

"Don't be sorry, it's me!"

"Hi, Theodor."

"Isn't it great? It looks like the communists are on the way out!"

"Well, they were becoming increasingly unpopular with the people."

"What's the matter? You look so glum!"

"I just made a confession today."

"A confession? Have you sinned?"

"I've been an informer for the Secret Police. I've been spying on the Democratic Party."

"You're kidding?"

"No, I wouldn't joke about something like that."

"Who did you confess to?"

"To the Democratic Party at a meeting."

"That was a brave thing to do."

"Brave – or foolish."

"Why did you become an informer?"

"I wanted to help the communists. I sympathise with their ideals."

"I forgive you for being an informer. None of us are saints."

"I guess you're right."

"Still, I'm not in the mood for misery. Let's celebrate the revolution in a bar!"

"Not now, Theodor."

"I won't take no for an answer," said Theodor, dragging Frank towards a bar.

A few hours later, the two men left the bar in order to return home. Soon Frank was outside the block of flats containing his one. He entered the building and shortly stepped into his home. He stood in the hall under the influence of alcohol.

"I'm home!" he said, then entered the kitchen.

"Hiya!" said Alexis, who was stirring a stew on the hob. "Well done, you bothered to come home in time for supper."

"Of course," said Frank. He walked over to Alexis, hugged her and kissed her on the cheek.

"What was that for?" she asked.

"For being you," said Frank, then he removed a small box from his pocket and gave it to Alexis.

"What's this, then?"

"Open it and find out."

"Frank! A bracelet! How lovely! You shouldn't have."

"Yes, I should! Put it on."

"All right. There…it fits," said Alexis, then kissed Frank on the cheek. "Why did you…wait a minute, what's up?"

"Nothing."

"Yes, there is. You're buttering me up."

"Don't be so suspicious."

"Something's happened, I can tell."

"Well…"

"Come on, spill the beans," said Alexis and they sat down on nearby chairs.

"I became an informer…for the Secret Police," said Frank.

"I can't believe it."

"It's true."

"Is that why you've been acting so strangely recently?"

"Yes. I didn't tell you in order to protect you."

"Huh! What a hero. What was the information about?"

"I was spying on the Democratic Party, on my university colleagues."

"Well done. I could never stand those creeps. Why did you do it?"

"I wanted to serve the Communist Party. I believe in their ideals of equality, public ownership, collective responsibility and so on."

"That's fair enough."

"It's not that simple."

"What's the problem?"

"I may lose my job. The university officials will frown upon an informer. It doesn't look good."

"So what? Get a job somewhere else."

"I might get a post at a local college."

"Problem solved. Now, let's eat. I'm starving."

Alexis served up the stew and the couple ate at the table. Later, they watched television, then retired to bed. Frank hoped the next day would be less difficult for him.

CHAPTER TWENTY ONE

It was the evening in a busy street full of cafes and bars. Theodor stood at a corner as people passed by, enjoying the night. Soon Frank approached his friend, whom he had arranged to meet there.

"Good evening," said Frank.

"Excellent! You made it," said Theodor.

"Let's go inside," said Frank, so they entered a cafe and walked up to the bar.

"Two ales, please," said Theodor.

"How was your day?" asked Frank.

"Fine, you know, I've been busy. How was yours?"

"Not so great. I had a meeting with the University Vice Chancellor. He's transferred me to a local college because of my involvement with the Secret Police. I'm not very popular at the University, so he's given me a fresh start."

"It's better than nothing."

"Two ales," said the barman.

"Thank you," said Theodor, handing over the money.

A man bumps into Frank, who is startled and says:"Hey, watch where you're going."

"Or else?" retorted the man, gruffly.

"Or else? Wait a minute...Krystof?"

"And you're Frank – the informer!"

"That's all over now. Just get out of our way," asserted Theodor.

"Why should I?" asked Krystof.

"I don't want any trouble in here. If you want to fight, go outside," said the barman.

Krystof grimaced, then left the cafe. He passed two young women who were giggling over a joke they had just heard. The cafe was busy with an assortment of customers.

"Thanks," said Frank.

"Don't mention it," said the barman, handling a glass.

Frank and Theodor found a table, then sat down. There was a picture on the wall next to the table of some farm workers ploughing a field. Frank hoped he would not experience more trouble owing to his time as an informer.

"That was a close shave," he said.

"Don't worry about it. He was drunk," said Theodor.

"It looked that way."

"Have you heard today's news?"

"Not yet."

"Things are going well. The Communist Party has given in to the protestor's demands for reform. They have formed a coalition government with the Democratic Party."

"That is good news. Do you still want to emigrate?"

"It depends. If the country changes for the better, I may wish to stay."

Outside, Alexis walked towards the cafe, feeling afraid and worried. Earlier, Frank informed her he would be drinking there. She entered the cafe, looked around, then walked over to Frank.

"Alexis, why have you come here? What's the matter?" he asked.

"Frank, something terrible has happened! You must come home!" she said.

Frank, Alexis and Theodor left the cafe and arrived outside the flat a while later. The word 'INFORMER' had been painted in red on the front door. It was an alarming sight for them.

"Damn," said Frank, scratching his head.

"What's going to happen to us?" asked Alexis.

"Nothing..." said Frank.

"What if they come to get us – tonight?" asked Alexis.

"They won't, it's just a prank," reassured Theodor.

"How do you know?" asked Alexis.

"You can stay at your mother's if it makes you feel any better," suggested Frank.

"Don't worry, I will," said Alexis.

"I think I've got some paint inside..." said Frank.

"That's good. Cover it over," said Alexis.

"We are living in turbulent times and people's emotions are bubbling over. Don't worry about this. Whoever did this is just trying to scare you," said Theodor.

"They have succeeded," said Alexis.

"I'll fetch the paint," said Frank, then entered the flat.

Marius left his flat, then noticed Alexis with Theodor, apparently troubled. He approached them, hoping to understand their anxiety. He wondered if he could assist them.

"Good evening, Alexis," he said, cautiously, but he managed to startle her.

"M – Marius! It's nice to see you," she said, stepping back.

Alexis stood between the neighbour and the front door, using her body to hide the word 'INFORMER'. She felt rather awkward, but held her ground. Marius was confused, but concerned.

"What's the matter? You seem tense," he continued.

"Nothing is the matter," said Alexis, firmly.

"Fair enough," said Marius, shrugging his shoulders."And who is this?"

"This is Theodor, the local scoundrel," said Alexis, managing a smile.

"Good evening," said Theodor and shook the neighbour's hand, warmly.

"Have you been watching the news? It's exciting, all this political upheaval," said Marius.

"Politicians? They're all the same to me," declared Alexis, with a shrug.

"Quite. I do hope the new Democratic Party will lower taxes and build more public toilets. There is a lack of them in Malvaria, as I'm sure you'll agree," said Marius.

"I hadn't noticed," said Alexis.

"Yes, I think you've hit on something there," agreed Theodor, nodding.

"Quite," said Marius.

Frank appeared at the doorway with the paint. He did not expect to see his neighbour, but found middle-aged people amusing. However, he did not wish to die before he grew old as lecturers received a generous pension.

"Frank! What are you doing?" asked Marius.

"I'm going to paint the door," replied Frank.

"It's a funny time to paint the door."

"We're funny people."

"Quite. Still. I must return to my wife. She will be wondering where I am. I just popped out because I could hear voices and I wanted to…"

"Be nosy," added Alexis.

"If you're hearing voices, I could refer you to a psychiatrist," said Frank.

"The one you're seeing?" inquired Marius.

"Marius! Get back in here!" ordered Marius's wife, standing at their doorway. She had brown eyes with grey, permed hair. She wore a woolly cardigan, plain blouse, knee length skirt plus slip on shoes and was in her fifties.

"Coming, darling," said Marius, then entered his flat with his grumpy wife.

"What a quaint man," commented Theodor.

"He's a nosy bastard," said Alexis.

"Did he see the word?" asked Frank as he began to paint over it on the front door.

"No, I stood in front of it," said Alexis, feeling relieved.

"Well done," said Frank.

"We don't want him asking questions and spreading rumours," said Alexis.

"He's not that bad, is he?" asked Theodor, inquisitively.

"He's worse," said Alexis.

"So, what's the plan?" inquired Theodor.

"After Frank has finished his masterpiece, I'm off to my mother's for the night," said Alexis.

"And then..." said Theodor.

"Don't tell me, you wish to return to the bar for another drink?" asked Alexis.

"No, not at all. You're scared so I'll stay with you," reassured Frank, touching Alexis's arm.

"I'm fine now, just about. I'll take a few things to my mother's. I'll be fine there," said Alexis.

"But..." said Frank.

"No buts. Enjoy the rest of the evening with Theodor. That's an order. We mustn't allow stupid people to spoil our lives," said Alexis.

"Fair enough. I'll join you at your mother's later," said Frank and finished painting the door.

Alexis entered the flat where she packed a few items to take to her mother's. When she was ready, she departed, then Frank and Theodor returned to the cafe. They purchased a couple of drinks, then sat at a table. By chance, Melissa, a little drunk, entered the premises where she approached the two friends.

"Theodor! I thought I recognized you!" she said and kissed him on both cheeks.

"Melissa! How are you?" asked Theodor, enjoying the encounter.

"I'm fine! Just fine! Hi Frank."

"Good evening," he said.

"Everything is going well with the Democratic Party. Hammond is going to have a meeting with the leader of the Communist Party tomorrow," said Melissa.

"Excellent," said Theodor, then he noticed the arrival of Reuben.

"There you are. I wondered where you were," said Reuben.

"Look who I've found," said Melissa.

"I see."

"Reuben's bought a new car! Come out and see it!"

"Don't show off."

"I like to show off! It's in my nature. Come on."

The four of them left the cafe, then walked around the corner. Here, they admired Reuben's red sports car with the roof down. Melissa was very excited.

"Isn't she wonderful?" she asked.

"The car is female?" inquired Frank, rather surprised.

"Of course she is," replied Melissa.

"How fast can she go?" asked Theodor, stepping around the motor car.

"Well above the speed limit," answered Reuben, proudly.

"What is she like to drive?" asked Theodor, looking at the interior.

"She handles like a dream. Get inside. I'll take you for a spin," said Reuben.

"You've been drinking?" inquired Theodor.

"Just the one. Ask Melissa. And Frank, no hard feelings," said Reuben, shaking the lecturer's hand.

"Thank you," said Frank, appreciatively.

They all entered the car, then sat on black, leather seats. Reuben drove off and toured around the city, enabling the passengers to enjoy the sights. They passed numerous important statues and monuments, reminding them of Malvaria's history.

"All these political changes are so exciting," said Melissa with the wind blowing in her face.

"You think so?" asked Frank.

"Yes, I do. The country needs to westernize, then I can buy designer clothes!"

"Is that all you think about – fashion?"

"Yes."

"Change isn't always for the better."

"Don't be so gloomy."

"The country won't change completely in the near future. The Communist Party is still supported by many people – the communists won't disappear."

"I guess you're right."

"Yes, Frank is a big fan of the communists," remarked Reuben, grinning."I oppose them because too much state control is bad for the economy. Free enterprise and competitiveness will lead to a more prosperous Malvaria, you wait and see."

"But the communists have focussed on making the economy more productive in the last decade," said Frank.

"But Frank, they have stifled political dissent," said Melissa.

"She's right. The government is too oppressive," said Reuben.

"We need a party who can unite the people, to bring about social harmony," said Theodor.

"Unity is an illusion, life is conflict. Do you agree, Frank?" asked Reuben.

"I believe in equality," said the lecturer.

"And I believe in rights. Besides, why should we trust a bunch of unelected, middle-aged men to run the country? It's absurd," said Reuben.

"Watch out!" cried Melissa, pointing ahead, where a car had halted.

Reuben slammed his foot on the break peddle and everyone in the car lunged forward.

"What are you playing at?" Reuben shouted at the driver ahead, who drove off."Sorry about that."

"Don't worry," said Melissa.

"We were discussing politics," said Frank.

"I believe in democracy," said Reuben, driving onwards.

"But do you know what democracy really means in the West? Capitalism, every man for himself, the rat race," said Frank.

"It's not that bad. Besides, we don't have true communism here. The economy is run by the government, not by the people so there's no collective control," said Reuben.

"The communists have principles," said Frank.

"But they don't believe in the freedom of speech, unlike the West, unlike me," said Reuben.

"I'm close to home now. Can you drop me off here, please? I want to collect some belongings before I join my wife," said Frank.

"No problem," said Reuben, stopping the car.

"Good night," said Frank, departing from the vehicle.

"See you," said Melissa, then Reuben drove off.

"I suppose he's off to supply the Secret Police with more information," said Reuben, giggling.

Frank walked down a street and checked his watch: it was 11pm. He turned a corner, then continued his journey home. Up ahead, a figure in a dark coat approached him. It was Krystof.

"Hey! It's you," he said, glaring at Frank.

"I beg your pardon?" asked Frank, looking up at the man.

"It's you! The informer."

"Get out of my way!"

"You're going nowhere! Not after I've finished with you!"

Krystof brandished a knife, then raised it in the air, about to strike. A passer by grabbed Krystof's hand, making the knife fall to the ground. Frank was stunned by this action. The passer by forced Krystof to the ground, holding him there. Frank wondered who had saved him: it was Austin.

"Now little man, I think you've had too much to drink tonight. I'm going to let you go and I want you to return home to sober up. Unless, of course, you want a bullet in your head," said Austin, aiming a gun at Krystof.

Austin released Krystof, who ran off. Frank, feeling shocked, watched his assailant disappear around a corner. Austin picked up the knife as a precaution.

"Frank, you just encountered one of the more colourful members of Drapov."

"You saved my life," said Frank.

"It's all part of the service."

"You know that man?"

"Yes, of course. The Secret Service knows everything."

"He's a mature student."

"Indeed. I heard him call you an informer."

"That's right...I admitted it to the Democratic Party at a meeting he attended."

"Frank, honesty is not always the best policy in Malvaria!"

"Well..."

"Never mind. Besides, I was on my way to your apartment. Let's walk."

"You know where I live? How come?"

"I have access to the appropriate files."

"I see. Someone daubed the word 'INFORMER' on our front door."

"That's disgraceful! The mentality of some people."

"It's understandable..."

"Rubbish! You had the ingenuity to cooperate with the authorities and some people are jealous. End of story."

"I had to take a teaching post at a local college because the University officials found out I was an informer."

"Well done. You turned your problems into opportunities."

"And you? What is your future?"

"For the first time in my life, I'm not sure. I could apply for a job in the police force, or seek a different avenue. I've always fancied myself as a gardener. What do you think?"

"Why not? And why have you come to see me?"

"I wanted to thank you for your co-operation, for your information. Your services have been greatly appreciated by myself and my superiors. We have reached the end of an era – and a new one has begun!"

"You sound like an historian."

"Well, it takes one to know one! Now, my business with you is complete. It is time for me to return home."

"Where do you live?"

"That's private."

"You know where I live."

"Tough luck, Frank. Some things will remain secret. Good night."

Austin walked off into the night and waved. Frank had a feeling he would not see him again, then returned home. He collected some belongings then joined Alexis at her mother's.

CHAPTER TWENTY TWO

It was the day time at Capital Square. The weather was sunny and breezy without a cloud in the sky. Theodor stood by a monument, waiting for Frank, who soon arrived.

"Hi," greeted Theodor.

"Good afternoon," said Frank.

"Have you and Alexis returned to your apartment?"

"Yes, we have."

"Has there been any more trouble?"

"No."

"I'm glad to hear it. Come on, I'm dying for a coffee."

"Caffeine addict!"

"Hypocrite!"

They walked down a street, then turned a corner. They approached a popular cafe with chatty customers seated around numerous tables outside. Once inside, the two friends stepped over to the bar.

"Two coffees, please," said Frank.

"Of course," said the bar man.

Behind the bar, a television was broadcasting the news. Frank and Theodor paid attention to it. A young, blond, female newsreader spoke:"Earlier today, the Communist government resigned and Hammond Martinek, leader of the Democratic Party, was elected as the president by a parliament dominated by communist deputies. Hammond is the first non-communist president for over 40 years."

"President Hammond. He'll become more big headed than ever!" said Frank.

"I think he'll do a good job," said Theodor.

"Let's hope so."

On the television, Hammond spoke:"I am honoured to have been voted as the President of Malvaria. I will proceed to democratize the country by holding free elections in the summer. I will do my best to improve Malvaria and look forward to your co-operation. This is an historical day and will not be forgotten. The country will continue to change but we must hold onto our traditional values."

"Here are your coffees, gentlemen," said the barman.

"Thank you," said Frank.

"I've had enough of politics. Let's sit down," said Theodor.

The two friends take their coffees over to a table where they sit down. Leopold entered the cafe and approached the two men. He appeared to be startled.

Good afternoon," he said.

"Leopold, I haven't seen you in a while," said Frank.

"No, I heard you were transferred to another teaching post after your confession."

"That is correct."

"I still can't believe what you did."

"Hey, give the man a break. He tried to help me escape to Germany," remarked Theodor.

"But I am young and believe in ideals – like truth and justice," said Leopold.

"You may well lose them once you've lived in the real world for a while."

"I will hold onto my ideals, no matter what."

"How are your studies?" asked Frank.

"They're fine, although your replacement knows the subject but can't teach so well," said Leopold.

"Such is life."

"Still, it's better than being taught by a traitor!"

Theodor stood up angrily. He was annoyed with the student and wanted to defend his friend. Loyalty was important to him.

"Listen kid, this is a time for reconciliation, not recrimination," he said.

"You think so?" asked Leopold.

"I do. We've all done contentious things, including you."

Hugh entered the cafe in a good mood. He looked around the place, then noticed his student friend. He walked over to him, smiling.

"There you are, Leopold," he said.

"You're late," said Leopold.

"Sorry, your highness. Hi there."

"Hi Hugh," said Frank.

"Leopold was just rebuking Frank for being an informer," explained Theodor.

"Is that so? Well, Leopold loves to moralize about people," said Hugh.

"There is a right and a wrong!" said Leopold.

"Have you told them about the library book?"

"Be quiet about that!"

"What's this about a library book?" asked Theodor.

"It's nothing..." said Leopold.

"Come on, now. I'm intrigued!"

"Now look what you've done!"

"Once Leopold returned a book back to the University Library two months late and refused to pay the fine," said Hugh.

"It was a lot of money," said Leopold.

"You ought to have returned it earlier," said Theodor.

"I forgot I had it!"

"What was the book about?"

"Moral philosophy."

"Leopold only paid the fine when the librarian warned him she would inform the head of the History Faculty if he didn't pay up!" said Hugh.

"I didn't have much money at the time," said Leopold.

"I'll forgive you for your transgression," said Theodor. "Still, you paid up in the end."

"Come on, let's drink outside," said Hugh.

"Good night," said Frank.

"Good night," said Hugh, then left the cafe with Leopold in order to drink at an empty table near the entrance.

"Students! They're the future!" exclaimed Theodor.

Frank and Theodor spent an hour in the cafe discussing the future of the country. Afterwards, they visited a bar down the same street. There was a band playing there who they listened to, then returned home.

CHAPTER TWENTY THREE

Six months passed and the first free elections for over forty years were held in Malvaria. As a result, the Democratic Party won significant majorities in both houses of parliament. The new government undertook the various tasks of transition, including the privatization of businesses, changing foreign policy and writing a new constitution.

It was the afternoon in Capital Park during a sunny and cloudy day. Theodor was excited as he clutched an envelope. Frank soon walked over to him with a bemused expression.

"Frank! Frank!" said Theodor, gleefully.

"What's going on? Why did you want to meet me here?" asked Frank, feeling puzzled.

"Look! Look at this!" said Theodor, waving the envelope.

"What is it? Have you won a prize?"

"No! Read it for heaven's sake!"

"All right! Keep your hat!" said Frank and began to read the letter."I see…it's from the friends of the Democratic Party in Germany…they still want you to emigrate."

"I know! It's great news."

"It sounds like you want to go."

"Too right! It's much easier to emigrate now the Democratic Party is in power."

"We'll miss you, Alexis and me."

"That's not a problem. You can visit me and vice versa. I'll keep in touch."

"Is there much employment where your friends live?"

"Yes. They are confident they can find me a job."

"That's good."

"Still, nothing is final yet. I'll have to fill in emigration papers from City Hall once more. What's the matter? You seem sad."

"I'm losing my drinking partner."

"Never mind. You'll have to take Alexis out more often."

"She doesn't drink."

"Don't worry, my friend, you'll think of something. Now then, let's head for the City Hall."

The two men walked down a few streets and passed a street performer juggling some multi-coloured balls in the air. They dropped some coins into his hat on the ground, then arrived at City Hall shortly afterwards. Theodor skipped up the stone steps to the entrance.

"Hurry up, slow coach!" he said to Frank, who trailed behind

"You're the one who wants to emigrate, not me!" declared Frank, frowning.

"There's no excuse for being unfit – or lazy!"

"Just wait until you reach my age!" said Frank, who was a little older than his friend and met him at the top of the steps."Here we go."

They entered City Hall where they walked over to the reception. Here the female receptionist was browsing through a brochure. She noticed the two men and addressed them courteously.

"Good afternoon, gentlemen. How may I help?" she asked.

"It's me again. Do you remember?" asked Theodor.

"I've met a lot of men in my time...Wait a minute, yes, I recall. You tried to emigrate last year, but were not permitted."

"That's right."

"And you tried to emigrate unlawfully, but were foiled!"

"How do you know?"

"When you work for the government, you hear many things on the grapevine."

"I'm going to attempt to emigrate lawfully this time."

"Of course. We now have a new government."

Hilda Page walked over to the reception. She recognized the two men and wondered what they wanted. She possessed a bemused expression.

"Mr Rushkin is putting himself first once again," she said, smiling.

"Mrs Page," said Theodor.

"The one and only."

"You're still here."

"Indeed."

"I thought you might have been promoted – or demoted."

"Some things don't change. The government recognizes a good worker. Still, it's a shame you're not remaining loyal to the country."

"I have my own plans."

"Evidently."

"We have new freedoms under a democratic government,"

"They shouldn't be abused."

"I am benefitting from them."

"What's the matter? I thought you would want to contribute to the country now we are a democracy."

"Well, I don't. What are you going to do? Lock me up?"

"I don't have the power to do that."

"We came for the emigration papers, not a confrontation," informed Frank.

"Very well, gentlemen. I will fetch the appropriate papers – for one person?" asked Hilda.

"Yes. I'm staying put."

"Bravo. Now wait a minute, " said Hilda, heading towards her office.

"She's not afraid to speak her mind," said Frank.

"Hilda has always been forthright in her opinions," said the receptionist, before Hilda returned with the papers.

"There you are. Fill them in and return them in the envelope provided," she said, handing the paper work to Theodor.

"Thank you very much," he said.

Theodor and Frank left City Hall, then descended the stone steps until they reached the pavement. A couple of cyclists passed by them on the road, travelling at a high speed. An elderly lady crossed the road, carrying her weekly groceries.

"I'm off to fill these in," explained Theodor, then the two men returned to their respective abodes.

CHAPTER TWENTY FOUR

A few days passed and Frank was to be found drinking at the bar in a cafe one evening. He noticed Krystof walk past the premises carrying a can of petrol. The nature student looked around and his behaviour was suspicious. Frank was concerned, drank up, then departed from the cafe. He followed Krystof, who walked with a stubborn sense of purpose, as he turned a few corners. Frank endeavoured to remain unseen, but continued in his pursuit of the student.

Krystof stopped outside a fine house, then looked behind, so Frank hid behind a parked car. Krystof smashed a front window to the house with the can, then poured petrol inside. Frank was alarmed. Krystof lit a match and set fire to the petrol inside the building. Frank stood up in anger.

"Hey, you maniac!" he shouted.

Krystof saw Frank, grinned and ran off. Frank sprinted over to the house, then knocked at the front door, but nobody answered. He ran around the side of the building and reached the back door. Here he smashed the back door window, unlocked the door, then entered the house. He found himself in the kitchen and entered the hall. The door to the room containing the fire was closed.

"Is anybody at home?" he shouted.

Nobody answered, so he climbed the stairs. Meanwhile, the fire raged in the front room. Frank reached the landing and arrived in front of a closed door. He burst into the room to see a man in bed. It was Austin.

"Austin! Wake up!" shouted Frank, leading the detective to stir, wake up and arise.

"Frank? What are you doing here?" asked Austin, sleepy and rather confused.

"Get out of bed! The house is on fire!"

"What?"

"Hurry! There's no time to lose!"

"The house is on fire? My God! We'd better leave."

Austin left his bed, realizing the urgency of the situation. He was dressed in his pyjamas. He had faith in Frank's ability to address the current dilemma.

"Follow me," said Frank, so they stepped onto the landing, descended the stairs and arrived in the hall."This way!"

Smoke had begun to fill the house. The two men left through the front door, relieved to be outside the burning building. Here they met two neighbours.

"We heard the window being smashed and someone shout," said Esther, a middle-aged woman who wore spectacles in front of her blue eyes. She had short, greying hair and wore a blouse, cardigan, knee length skirt plus well worn shoes.

"Are you all right?" asked Miles, a man near to fifty who had hazel eyes and was partly bald. He wore a patterned jumper, straight trousers plus sensible shoes.

"Just about," replied Austin, who valued their concern.

"I'll call for a fire engine," said Miles, observing the flames in the house.

"That's a sensible idea," said Frank, then Miles re-entered his house next door.

"Did you see who did it?" asked Austin, as curious as ever.

"Yes, it was Krystof, the guy who tried to stab me the other night. Do you remember?"

"Him? Yes, I do."

"It looks like he tried to pick on you, instead."

"Indeed. He found out my address, assuming he knew I lived here."

"Never mind. The fire engine should be here soon," said Esther, offering some comfort.

After a while, the fire engine arrived and managed to eventually extinguish the fire. Frank called the police, who drove over so that he and Austin could give statements detailing events that night. Austin spent the night at Esther and Miles's abode, whilst Frank returned home. The following day, the police arrested Krystof having acquired his address from the University and questioned him. Under pressure, he confessed to the crime: he wanted revenge against Austin after the detective protected Frank from the earlier knife attack. Krystof had trailed Austin home in order to ascertain his personal address, then planned the arson. Krystof was to be held in police custody until a court case was arranged.

CHAPTER TWENTY FIVE

It was midday outside the block of flats where Frank lived. Theodor looked up at the building, then entered and ascended the stairs, smiling. He reached the door to Frank's flat, which he knocked. The lecturer opened the door.

"I have good news, my friend," said Theodor, beaming.

"You've found a cure for the common cold?" asked Frank, inquisitively.

"No, much better than that! I've been permitted to emigrate to Germany!"

"Well done!"

They hugged, then Alexis appeared in the doorway. She was amused by the spectacle before her and wondered what the cause was.

"What's all this male bonding for?" she asked.

"I'm emigrating to Germany," disclosed Theodor.

"Well done."

"I received the papers this morning."

"Come inside," invited Frank, so Theodor entered the flat.

"When do you plan on leaving?" asked Alexis, once they were inside the living room.

"As soon as possible, in the next few weeks. I'll hire a van for my belongings plus a driver," said Theodor, as they sat down.

"How will Frank cope without you?" inquired Alexis.

"I'm sure he'll manage."

"He'll have to find a new drinking partner. Still, he's made new friends at the college."

"I see. And what is your news?"

"I witnessed a maniac trying to burn down a house the other night. The police caught him and they're confident he'll be convicted for arson. I may have to go to court as a witness," said Frank.

"Indeed. And how are things with you?" asked Theodor.

"The usual. Domestic chores and looking after Frank," replied Alexis.

"Of course. He needs to be looked after."

The trio talk for a while, discussing Theodor's plans for his new life in Germany. Frank prepared a light lunch, which they enjoy. Later on, Theodor returned home.

Krystof was prosecuted in court for arson. Frank was present as a witness and testified, along with Austin. Krystof was awarded a five year prison sentence.

CHAPTER TWENTY SIX

It was the early morning outside the block of flats where Theodor lived. The sun was rising, heralding a new day. Theodor, Frank, Alexis, Reuben and Melissa stood near to a white van. The driver closed the back doors to the vehicle.

"This is it, then. The final farewell," said Frank, then hugged his friend.

"Don't worry. I'll write to you," said Theodor. He hugged and kissed Alexis.

"Don't forget to ring us," she said.

"Good luck," said Reuben. They hugged.

"Goodbye. We'll miss you!" said Melissa. They hugged and kissed.

"I'll miss you too!" said Theodor, then noticed the driver entered the van. "It looks like it's time to go."

Theodor entered the van where he sat in the passenger seat. He felt sad to leave his friends behind, but looked forward to the future. He waved, then the van drove off. His friends waved as the vehicle departed. Theodor recalled his life in Malvaria: his parents, who tragically died in a car accident in his twenties, the schools he attended, his first love, the insurance broker he worked for, his social life and so on. He had mixed feelings about the past, but he did not wish to spend too long reflecting upon his history. After a while, his mind returned to the present and he felt excited about the opportunities available in Germany.

Meanwhile, a man lay on his bed in a prison cell. He read a book entitled Moral Philosophy. The reader was Krystof.

Printed in Poland
by Amazon Fulfillment
Poland Sp. z o.o., Wrocław